# WATER UNDER BRIDGES

Pink Bean Series - Book 5

HARPER BLISS

**ALSO IN THE PINK BEAN SERIES**
This Foreign Affair
Everything Between Us
Beneath the Surface
No Strings Attached

**OTHER HARPER BLISS BOOKS**
In the Distance There Is Light
The Road to You
Far from the World We Know
Seasons of Love
Release the Stars
Once in a Lifetime
At the Water's Edge
French Kissing: Season Three
French Kissing: Season Two
French Kissing: Season One
High Rise (The Complete Collection)

Copyright © 2017 by Harper Bliss

Cover picture © Depositphotos / pproman

Cover design by Caroline Manchoulas

Published by Ladylit Publishing – a division of Q.P.S. Projects Limited - Hong Kong

ISBN-13 978-988-78013-0-6

All rights reserved. Unauthorised duplication is prohibited. This is a work of fiction. Any resemblance of characters to actual persons, living or dead, is purely coincidental.

All rights reserved.

No part of this book may be reproduced in any form or by any electronic or mechanical means, including information storage and retrieval systems, without written permission from the author, except for the use of brief quotations in a book review.

*To my wife (for putting the bliss in **Harper Bliss** on a daily basis)*

## Chapter One

As far as first days at new jobs went, this one had been easygoing for Mia. Kristin hadn't hired her to brew coffee; Mia was here for far loftier goals. Expansion. A second coffee shop in another part of the city. Obtaining a liquor license. Turning the Pink Bean *brand* into much more than the friendly neighborhood coffee shop it stood for today.

"Great product," she said to Kristin after taking a sip from her coffee. Strong and black. For someone who had just become manager of a coffee shop, Mia didn't truly believe all the fancy coffee drinks were necessary. What was wrong with plain old regular coffee? That was how she liked it. But she wouldn't have this new job if not for the fancier beverages which had a much higher margin than simple black coffee.

Tomorrow morning—bright and early—Mia was expected to handle the first barista shift of the day alongside Josephine, to whom she hadn't even been properly introduced. She had suggested it herself, favoring a hands-on approach and learning the ins and outs of the coffee shop business from actually working in one. The only part she wasn't very enthusiastic about was the starting time of her duties at 6:30 a.m.

"Hello, hello," Sheryl said as she entered the Pink Bean from the back room.

Kristin and her partner had interviewed Mia together for the position, so Mia had already been formally introduced. After the interview, which had been relaxed and free of the usual corporate stiffness, Mia had wanted the job so badly, she'd had to stop herself from going back in and pleading her case all over again. It was the vibe of the place. Not only the extreme gay-friendliness—or perhaps she should call it straight-friendliness—but the way the two of them were together. It gave her hope for better times in her own personal life. And the number of lesbians that must frequent the place. Mia didn't know the neighborhood very well, but even on the way over from the train her gaydar had pinged several times. The lesbian density wasn't as high as in Newtown, but the women here were different. And Mia could do with a new stomping ground.

"I know we hired you to help Kristin, but that doesn't mean she's allowed to boss you around too much." Sheryl kissed Kristin on the cheek. "She can be like that sometimes."

Kristin gave Sheryl a look, then refocused her attention on Mia. "Don't mind her. Sometimes she doesn't know when not to say something." Kristin shot Mia a warm smile, her eyes narrowing with glee and the skin around them crinkling up.

"I look forward to getting to know you better, Mia, but now I have to dash. Professorial duties are calling." She tipped a finger to her forehead and stopped at the counter where Josephine handed her a takeaway coffee she hadn't even had to order.

"Jo, can you join us for a minute?" Kristin asked.

"Sure. Refills?"

"No, that's all right," Kristin said.

Mia could have done with a refill but Kristin had the sort of insistent tone of voice she instinctively didn't want to argue with.

Kristin introduced Mia to Jo as *the new Pink Bean manager* and Jo to Mia as *the Pink Bean's longest and hardest-working employee with the voice of an angel*.

"I guess that makes you my new boss then," Josephine said. "So we'd best try to get along."

"You should really come to the next open mic night," Kristin said. "Jo will be singing and blow you away in the process. We're lucky to have her on our tiny stage once every two months these days, that's how in demand she is."

"Please, Kristin." Josephine waved her off. "You know how easily I blush."

A customer walked in and Kirstin got up. "You girls get acquainted. I'll take care of this."

Mia took the opportunity to study Josephine's face. She couldn't immediately place it, but something about her was beginning to look familiar. "Wait a minute. You're not Josephine Greenwood, are you?"

"The one and only. Why do you ask?"

"Er, because of this." Mia fished her phone out of her back pocket and scrolled to the WhatsApp message that contained the music file her friend Pat had sent her a few weeks ago. She tapped play and a powerful, impressive voice boosted from her phone's inadequate speakers. "Is this you?" She glanced at Josephine's face.

"Sounds like me. Where did you get this?"

"A friend sent it to me. She went to one of your gigs and made this recording. Sent it to all of us, that's how blown away she was by your voice. I could only agree." Mia gave

Josephine a wide smile. "It's an honor to be working with you."

"I'll sing you a tune once in a while." Everything about Josephine smiled.

"If you don't mind me asking—why are you working here? There's so much buzz about you in Sydney right now. You're about to blow up."

"Very simple. I need the money," Josephine said matter-of-factly. "Singing in student pubs doesn't pay that well."

Mia couldn't help herself. The question that worked its way from her brain to her mouth in record time was out before she could think about it. "Do you have someone looking out for your interests?"

"I have Jimmy."

"Who's Jimmy?"

"The guy playing guitar on that clip you just heard."

"Your guitar player is your manager?"

"He's not *my* guitar player and he's not my manager either. He takes care of all the bookings and the admin stuff, for which I'm very grateful."

Mia didn't know how to go about this. Tact had never been one of her strong suits. "The fact that I have this clip on my phone says so much. I don't usually know about new music, let alone about local bands or singers, but I do know about *you*, Josephine. You're on the verge of something. Just playing that ten-second clip gave me goosebumps."

"It's still just a hobby," Josephine said.

"My guess is it won't be for much longer. Your voice is too heavenly to keep it from the masses." Mia smiled at her new colleague.

Josephine tilted her head and painted a soft smile on her face. "Thank you for the kind words. I approve of the buttering up to your brand new co-worker strategy."

"I mean every word of it." Mia was starting to love the Pink Bean and its employees more by the second.

"To tell you the truth, I've had several offers for management and I think I am a little aware of the buzz, but I have so much going on right now, I don't even know where my head is most days. I probably shouldn't say this, but my mornings here are by far the most relaxing hours of my day. I can do this on autopilot and have a chat with the regulars, but the second I walk out of that door at lunch time, it's mayhem." She sent Mia an apologetic smile. "I think what I need most of all is a life coach. Or an assistant. Neither of which I have the money to pay for."

"Jo," Kristin said with a raised voice from behind the counter. "Amber and co are arriving. I'm going to need a hand."

"We'll talk more later," Mia said. "But if you ever need me to cover for you here, just ask."

"Thanks, Mia." Josephine got up and reached for their empty coffee cups.

Mia held up her hand. "I've got these." She gathered the cups from the table and stacked them in the dishwasher.

She watched Kristin and Josephine work in perfect tandem. A group of three very attractive women had just placed an order of *their usual* and was making its way to a table by the window.

"Mia, come meet some people you will see in here every day," Kristin said. "They're part of the furniture, really." She handed Mia a mug of green tea and carried two cups of coffee over to the table, gesturing for Mia to follow her.

"Ladies, please meet the brand new Pink Bean manager, Mia Miller. Mia, this is Amber, who will be having the tea." Kristin nodded at the woman with the ginger curls tied into a high ponytail. Mia set the tea down in front of her and put on her widest smile. "She runs the yoga studio down the street along with her best friend Micky, whose favorite drink is a cappuccino." Kristin set down the cappuccino in front of the dark-haired woman. "And a short black for Louise," Kristin said and winked at the youngest woman of the bunch and, to Mia's tastes, the most interesting looking. Dark, piercing eyes. Straight black hair that fell to her shoulders. And that skin. Not quite dark and not quite pale. Christ, maybe she should take up yoga lessons.

"It's a pleasure to meet you, ladies." Mia tried to imprint their names into her brain. She wouldn't have any trouble remembering Louise's.

"Micky used to work here, until she decided that yoga was more her thing than coffee," Kristin said with a grin on her face. "And Amber stole her from me."

"If I remember correctly, dear Kristin, I was the one who gave her to you in the first place," Amber said.

"Excuse me," Micky said. "Nobody gave me to or stole me from anyone. I'm quite capable of making my own choices, thank you very much." She painted a stern expression on her face. "That's not to say that I don't miss my buddy Jo behind the counter and my wonderful ex-boss, of course." Micky craned her neck and gave Josephine a wave.

"So you all work at Glow?" Mia asked. The flyers near the door of the Pink Bean were hard to miss. She was mainly interested in finding out what Louise's position was, although the tights and tank top did give it away somewhat.

"Glow *is* the three of us," Amber said. "Louise just started a few weeks ago as an instructor. Micky handles the admin side of things. I basically had to hire her because she, her partner Robin, and her ex-husband invested the bulk of the money in our tiny but wonderful studio."

"And made all your dreams come true," Micky added.

Louise sat stiffly saying nothing and, it seemed to Mia, avoiding her gaze altogether. Maybe she was still getting used to her new employers. Mia knew all about it. She would send her a look of encouragement if only the woman would glance in her direction.

"It's nice to meet you," Amber said. "Odds are you'll be seeing lots of us."

"I look forward to it." Mia smiled widely and again, in vain, tried to find Louise's gaze. A challenge. She was up for that.

## Chapter Two

*Mia Miller.* Louise couldn't believe it. Just when things had started going her way again. She'd found a great job very close to her parents' house. She lived and breathed yoga and Amber was the same, and therefore a dream to work for. Micky was a hoot and she and Amber often formed a double act that had Lou in stitches when they went out for after-work drinks. She'd been coming to the Pink Bean for a while now and she liked the vibe of the place, and often came here between classes to relax, have a coffee and read a book. And now Mia Miller had turned up out of nowhere to ruin her life once again.

Of course Mia hadn't recognized her. Or if she had, she'd certainly hidden it well. No, if she had remembered who Lou was, there would have been at least a glimmer of recognition between them. And whereas Mia's face hadn't exactly remained blank, there was no sign of her having any idea who Lou was. Which was good, Lou guessed. She didn't want to drag up the past—especially not that dreadful part of it—and have an awkward conversation in the Pink Bean, which now no longer could be her place of sanctuary. Of all the people in Sydney, why did Kristin have to hire Mia? Oh well, Lou would have to spend more time at the studio then, or go home between classes. Did Kristin say Mia was the new manager? If so, maybe she had an office somewhere in the back and wouldn't show her face too much in the shop.

"You look like you've seen a ghost, Lou," Amber said. "What's wrong?"

Kristin and Mia had walked off and sat talking at a table a few feet away. Lou could hear snatches of Mia's voice when she talked and, after all these years, it still sent an icy chill down her spine.

"Nothing. Not feeling too well today. You know."

Lou had only been working for Amber for a month, but she already knew her well enough to know Amber would never leave it at that. Her only hope was that Micky would return swiftly to their table after her chat with Jo, so they could change the topic of conversation. But Micky seemed deeply engaged in whatever she and Jo were chattering and giggling away about, so it was just her and Amber at the table, and the silence spreading between them, needing to be filled.

"Mia and I went to the same school. It's a bit of a shock seeing her here."

"Oh. Yeah, you did look like you were genuinely surprised there for a moment." Amber examined Lou's face for a second longer, then averted her gaze—surely because she remembered Lou had told her a few weeks ago how uncomfortable it could make her feel when people stared at her for too long. Even well-intentioned, kind people like Amber.

Amber's inherent, blatant kindness was what had drawn Lou to Glow in the first place. She was hooked after her first class with Amber, because they obviously subscribed to the same principles of yoga—the non-trendy, open-minded school of thought on which all yoga principles were founded. Sadly, especially in a city like Sydney, many instructors liked to ignore these and preferred to focus on which latest fad could get them a higher member count and which brand of yoga pants they could sell those new members after class.

As soon as Amber had announced at the end of a particularly invigorating vinyasa class that she was looking for an instructor to join her, Lou had grabbed the opportunity. And now here she sat.

"Don't worry about it." She flashed Amber her most convincing smile, hoping it was enough to trick Amber into believing what she said was true. Amber with the sixth sense for when someone was feeling a little off kilter. Some mornings, when Lou arrived at Glow after a bad night's sleep, caused by the circumstances which had led her to end up in her old room at her parents' house, Amber would cast one glance at her and ask, "Bad night?" Before Lou had even said a single word. "It was a long time ago and she obviously didn't recognize me. It's not as if we were close or anything." An understatement if there ever was one.

Micky returned to the table and said, "Jo tells me Mia has an MBA. Meaning she possesses valuable business knowledge neither you nor I do. Should I ask her about that online advertising problem? Maybe it's just something silly we've been missing."

Amber pondered this for a moment. "I guess it doesn't hurt to ask, but make sure to offer her enough free classes in return for her counsel."

"In return she will get a few invaluable pointers about working at the Pink Bean. She will sort of be taking my place, after all. A position I held for quite some time."

*Oh great*, Lou thought. Just like that the conversation had drifted back to Mia. Whatever business conversation Amber and Micky were planning to conduct with her, she hoped it wouldn't bring Mia into Glow—and she hoped even more that Mia wasn't the yoga type. Lou was unsure of her reaction if Mia showed up to one of her classes.

"Yes, Micky, you are a true wunderkind. It took you a long time to get there, but here you are at last, at the tender age of forty-six. Part of the work force. Making the economy grow. Making Glow run like clockwork."

"Speaking of clockwork. I should really get back. And so should you, Amber. Your next class is an hour away, Lou, so if you would be so kind as to invite Mia to a free yoga class at a time of her choosing, and slip her my number while you're at it."

"What?" How did Lou get involved in asking Mia for anything at all? She hadn't even opened her mouth.

"Besides, you might get lucky. She was making eyes at you the entire time she and Kristin stood here earlier. You didn't notice?"

"They went to school together," Amber said, making Lou doubt the existence of her sixth sense. "Maybe she did recognize you, Lou."

"I'm pretty sure she didn't," Lou said with a small voice. "And I would appreciate it if I didn't have to run your errands, Micky."

Micky knitted her brows together. "What's gotten into you?"

"She's right, Micky." Amber came to her rescue. "We should ask Mia ourselves." She rose. "But now we really have to go. See you later, Lou."

Lou breathed in and out deeply, feeling as if she'd dodged a bullet, even if it had meant being rude to Micky and in front of Amber no less. She was still trying to make an excellent impression on her new bosses and talking back like that was probably not the best way to do that. But Lou would be damned if she'd do Micky's bidding on this. If it had been anyone else, of course, she would have gladly offered them a free lesson and given them information on the benefits of yoga, but not Mia Miller. Anyone but her.

Lou sneaked a glance at her. She allowed her gaze to drift to the table a few feet away from her for just a fraction of a second but, of course, just then, Mia looked up from her conversation with Kristin, and sent her the most excruciating smile. It was a well-meant smile, Lou was sure about that. But it was a little late for good intentions. Besides, Mia still had no clue of who she was. Lou couldn't help but wonder what Mia would say if she did.

Lou didn't smile back but instead gathered her belongings and headed out.

"Leaving already?" Jo asked. "I was getting ready to prepare your second caffeine shot of the morning."

"I have some errands to run before my next class." Lou rushed past the counter without asking Jo when she would find the time for class again. It had been a while since she'd last seen her on a mat.

## Chapter Three

"Do you have time for lunch in your busy schedule some time this week?" Mia asked Jo. "We're going to be working together so I'd like to invite you."

"How about a quick bite now?" Josephine hung her apron on the hook of the back door. "I'm starving and off duty."

"That would be great."

"I'm meeting my partner Caitlin and our publisher here in an hour anyway, so it suits me just fine."

"Your publisher?" Mia continued to be amazed by Josephine.

"Caitlin and I are writing a book together."

"Is there anything you don't do?" Mia asked.

"A great many things." Josephine shot her a wink and they went back into the shop to fetch some food and find a table.

Once they'd sat down and Mia had had time to parse Josephine's words, she said, "You really are a Jill of all trades."

"That's multitasking for you. Singing a tune while

brewing a cup of joe while thinking about the next chapter in our book *and* my dissertation."

"How do you juggle all of that?" Mia was beginning to understand Josephine's earlier sigh of desperation better.

"Not very well." She picked up her sandwich but paused before biting into it. "Do you have a girlfriend? I don't mean to be presumptuous, but I am getting a bit of a vibe off you."

Mia was really beginning to like her new colleague. "That vibe you got was correct. I'm out and proud and… very much single."

"I was single for the longest time. Then I met Caitlin, who is quite literally the woman of my dreams, and now that I'm with her I feel like I don't have nearly enough time to spend with her."

"At least you're writing a book together."

"Oh yes, I get to sit in on a publisher meeting. I hate meetings. Even if they're about a book I'm co-writing with my partner. I think all meetings should be canceled for all time."

"I hear you. That's one of the reasons I've been so excited about this job. Big corporations drive me nuts with all their meetings and management structure and hierarchy."

"You'll love this place then. Kristin and Sheryl are really great people. Not just as bosses. They're very kind and will look out for you." Josephine shot her a grin. "And I see you've met some of the regulars already."

"Yes." She paused for a second to conjure up their names. "Amber, Micky and Lou."

"Amber and Micky are best friends and have been coming here for years. Lou is new to the neighborhood."

"So you don't know her very well then?" Mia might as well try to get some information about Lou out of Josephine.

"A little. We have the odd conversation as one does at a coffee shop. She's quite reserved, much more so than Micky and Amber. Which is normal, I guess, since she only just started working for them. I've done a couple of her yoga classes and she's a great teacher. A bit insecure at times, perhaps, but I'm guessing those are just beginner's nerves. Do you practice yoga?"

Mia hadn't expected that much information to come her way so swiftly. "Just occasionally in front of my TV, following YouTube videos. I wouldn't exactly call it a practice. More like having a go at what everyone else is doing these days."

"I never practiced before, but Amber gave me some private lessons and subsequently won me over. We should go together some time."

"Give me some time to buy an outfit first," Mia joked.

"Sure, but if Amber asks, don't tell her you're waiting until you've found the perfect pants. You're bound to get a lecture if you do."

"I'll keep that in mind." Mia hesitated, but she was keen to know the answer to her next question. "Are they all... lesbians then?"

Josephine snickered. "Amber and Micky surely are. You'll meet their better halves soon enough. I don't know about Louise, but my money is on yes… or at least very likely."

"You haven't seen her with anybody?"

"No. Not someone she would have a romantic connection with, anyway." Josephine studied Mia's face. "Do I detect some interest?"

Mia shrugged. "I might need to take up yoga."

"She's in here every day so you should soon find out." Josephine leaned over the table. "If you can't find love in the Pink Bean, you won't find it anywhere." She gave a chuckle. "I met Caitlin here. Micky met Robin here. Working behind that counter will make you a veritable babe magnet."

Mia leaned back. "Is that right? There's power in that apron, heh?"

"You wouldn't know it at first, but oh yes." Josephine burst out into a full-on chuckle. "Speaking of babes." Her lips widened into the brightest smile. "There's Caitlin."

Mia narrowed her eyes. "That's Caitlin James."

"My thoughts exactly when I first saw her walk in here, but sorry, she's already taken." Josephine rose and waited for Caitlin to arrive at their table.

"Hey, babe." Caitlin ignored Mia completely, curved her arms around Josephine's waist, and kissed her on the lips for long seconds. "I'm early." Only then did she cast a glance in Mia's direction. They were obviously still very much in the honeymoon period of their relationship, what with how they were still all over each other in public.

"You must be Mia," Caitlin said. "Sheryl told me all about you."

Mia wondered what Sheryl had said about her. She rose and shook Caitlin's hand. Mia had read one of her books and had been thoroughly impressed. She'd had no idea that when Josephine mentioned her partner Caitlin, it was actually author and feminist icon Caitlin James, even though Josephine had mentioned that they were writing a book together.

"Pleasure to meet you, Miss James."

"Miss James?" Caitlin sucked her bottom lip into her mouth for a split second. "No." She shook her head. "It's bad enough my girlfriend is twenty years younger than me and makes me feel old on a daily basis. My name is Caitlin."

"It's okay, babe. So far you haven't had much trouble keeping up," Josephine said and kissed Caitlin on the cheek.

They all sat down and Mia was feeling a little bowled over by the sheer number of lesbians she had met since arriving at her new job that morning. Darlinghurst really was where it was at these days. She should consider leaving her flat above the fish and chip shop off King Street and move to this swanky, lady-loving hood, but Kristin would have to give her a raise first, and she'd only just started.

"I'll leave you ladies to it." It was clear that Josephine hadn't been lying when she said she didn't get to see enough of her partner. She'd only had eyes for Caitlin since the minute she'd walked in. Mia considered that if she was in a relationship with Caitlin James, she would most likely feel the same way.

But Mia was single. A few women had piqued her interest in the past couple of months, but they had only been mild blips on her radar. No earthquake had made her shake in her boots. No woman had made her want to burst out of her skin with the desire to know her better. Except perhaps Louise the yoga teacher this morning, although she had been rather standoffish.

"Don't be silly, Mia," Caitlin said. "We're going to get to know each other rather well so we might as well get a head start."

## Chapter Four

After Lou's Thursday night yoga class, which Phil had started attending religiously since Lou had become an instructor, they headed to his and his partner Jared's place, which was located two houses down from the Pink Bean.

"I hear they have big plans for this place," Phil said when they walked past. "I wouldn't mind if it was open late so I could hop in for a decaf with my favorite yoga instructor after class."

"And deprive me of hanging out with your lovely husband and two adorable children? Nu-uh," Lou said.

"Said children better be in bed by the time I put my key in the lock. I need my peace and quiet after you tried so hard to stretch and relax me."

Lou taught an easy-going yin class as her last one of the day on Thursdays, and she was feeling the effects of it as well. Or perhaps it was her lack of sleep which had been accumulating of late. Walking past the Pink Bean made her think of Mia Miller again. She took a deep breath and tried to push the thought away, knowing very well that whatever she resisted would only try harder to persist in her mind. She had been able to avoid the Pink Bean for the last few days, although she had walked past earlier that morning and seen Mia behind the counter, smiling widely—a smile that hid a multitude of sins.

"You know they'll want their Auntie Lou to give them a good night kiss. That's what Thursdays are for."

"Just don't go putting any ideas into their head about staying up any longer than they already have. They'll be unbearable tomorrow morning if they stay up too late tonight. And then Auntie Lou won't be around to make it all better."

As soon as Phil and Lou entered the house, Jared walked toward them with a finger pressed to his lips. "They're sleeping already. It's a miracle."

"Oh my god," Phil mouthed.

"Do you want me to leave?" Lou asked, keeping her voice very quiet as well.

"Of course not, honey," Jared said with his full voice.

*They* were their four-and-a-half-year-old twins Toby and Yasmine who could make so much noise just between the two of them, Lou had, on more than one occasion, excused herself from their presence because it was just too loud. She couldn't take it. Something she would need to work on because Lou wanted to have children herself. It had been one of the big points of contention between her and Angie—one of many. But Lou was somehow convinced that any child she would produce would be incapable of making the kind of noise Toby and Yasmine did. Noise was not in her nature, so it wouldn't be in her children's. *Yeah right*. Phil was one of the quietest guys she knew, whereas his kids were the opposite.

"The wine is chilled and the kids are in bed," Jared said. "Time for a drink with Auntie Lou."

"She keeps emailing me," Lou said. "I received another one just this morning." She thought about the email Angie had sent her, and the one before, and the one before. "She keeps *saying* that she screwed up and that she shouldn't have let me go and that it's all her fault, but has she taken the time to show up in Sydney to tell me this to my face?" Lou shook her head. "No, because she doesn't have time for that. And that's exactly the point." She expelled a sigh. "I think she's sending these emails to make herself feel better about what happened. To absolve herself of the guilt that comes with a break up. To be able to face the facts now that I've actually gone."

Phil tapped a fingertip against her glass. "This is empty and you know what that means."

"I finished my wine so I should stop whining." Lou was glad for the limit Phil had set her a few months ago, when she was still deep in the throes of heartache. Because venting was good, but everything needs limits. She pushed her glass of wine forward. "Hit me up again and change the subject."

Jared refilled all their glasses, emptying the bottle. Lou knew that after this glass she would go home. One shared bottle on Thursdays had become a comforting ritual.

"The Pink Bean has a new barista," Jared said. "I was hoping they would hire a hot guy for once, even though deep down I knew those lesbians would never go for it. But have you seen her, Lou? She's the kind of hot that makes a dyed-in-the-wool queer guy like me turn my head."

Lou nearly spurted out her wine. She put down her glass and didn't say anything.

"Lou?" Phil prodded. "Are you okay?"

Lou took a deep breath. She had believed she would never have to speak of this again. That the box she had put that awful, demeaning chapter of her life in could remain closed forever.

"Yes. I have seen her and have actually met her." Lou tried to keep her voice steady. "Her name is Mia. Mia Miller."

She peered at Phil, one of her oldest friends, trying to gauge if he would remember. Lou hadn't uttered the name Mia Miller in a very long time. She hadn't needed to anymore. Both she and Phil had lived a lifetime between then and now.

Phil's eyes went wide. "Not *that* Mia Miller?" he asked.

"The one and only." Lou's voice broke a little, which she hated herself for. Mia shouldn't still hold this power over her. But it had been the shock of coming face to face with her when she least expected it that had been the worst of it.

"And who is this Mia Miller if I may be so ignorant to ask?" Jared said.

"She used to—" Phil started, undoubtedly trying to spare Lou from having to say the words out loud, but Lou put a hand on his forearm and he stopped talking.

"We both went to Queen Mary. She was a year above me and had quite the reputation for stirring up trouble and bullying. Then she had to redo her last year, putting us in the same class, and she promptly found a new target for her cruel jokes."

Jared quirked up his eyebrows. "You?"

Lou nodded. "I was never the most popular girl in school. I was never going to be with the color of my skin in a predominantly white school. But I got on. Got good grades. Moved around semi-comfortably in my small circle of friends. Then Mia Miller came along, set her sights on me, ruined my last year of high school and destroyed my spirit along the way." Lou tried to gain strength from drawing in another deep breath. "It was a long time ago."

"It doesn't matter that it was a long time ago." Jared tried to find her gaze.

"I have hated Mia Miller with a vengeance since I was seventeen years old. I've had revenge fantasies. I envisioned her ending up in jail or leading a miserable life somewhere, repenting for all she put me through when she was younger, but I never, ever expected to run into her in my local coffee shop just as I'm trying to put my life back together again."

"Did she say anything when you were introduced?" Phil asked.

"No. She had no idea who I was. For which I'm glad, by the way."

"So you're not going to confront her?" Jared asked.

"God no. Why would I do that?" Lou swallowed a large gulp of wine.

"Because you'll be seeing a lot of her. Your lot are always hanging out at the Pink Bean. It's like lesbian central in Darlinghurst, but a much classier version of what I ever could have imagined that to be," Jared joked. "You can't see her almost every day and walk around with this grudge. It will eat you alive. You should get it out into the open. Make her apologize."

Lou shook her head vehemently. "No. What's an apology going to do for me now, anyway? It's much too late for that. I'll just ignore her as best I can. I'll avoid the Pink Bean for now. I heard Micky say she's in training, getting ready to set up a new branch elsewhere. So it's only temporary. It can be done."

"Oh, Lou. Are you sure?" Phil asked. "Are you going to be all right?"

She smiled. "I'll be fine." Of course she would be fine. She didn't have much choice, just like she hadn't had any choice but to get on with things fifteen years ago, when Mia had been her daily tormentor. When she took it all in silence and never let anyone see her cry—apart from her father.

"Do you want us to boycott the Pink Bean as long as she's a barista there?" Jared asked.

"Of course not. I don't want you to change anything about how you conduct yourselves."

"Is there anything we can do to help at all?" Phil asked.

Lou shook her head again. "I really don't see what can be done about it. I'll just need to be patient and hope Kristin decides to open that new branch soon."

"Just to be clear," Jared said, "it *is* okay for Phil and me to go to the open mic tomorrow evening? Josephine Greenwood is performing and I have a feeling we won't be able to hear her sing at our local coffee shop for much longer."

"Jared. Come on," Phil said. "We don't have to go."

"It's fine. You guys go."

"Are you sure you don't want to come?" Jared asked. "There's safety in numbers, you know?"

"I'll have a quiet night in." Lou said.

"No chance of that. Remember who will be staying at your house?" Jared said.

"All the better for it," Lou said, wondering if she wasn't overreacting and letting this bully from her past exert too much influence on her present life. She was giving up a night out with her friends in order to stay away from Mia. Mia wouldn't be the only person there—maybe she wasn't even going. The whole point of the evening was to watch Josephine perform. Mia had nothing to do with it. "Actually, you know what? I'm too old to let the likes of Mia Miller dictate what I do with my life. I want to hear Jo sing. To hell with Mia."

"Hear, hear," Phil said, and held up his near-empty glass.

## Chapter Five

Mia could hardly believe the number of people that had shown up for Josephine's gig. Kristin called it an open mic night, but no one else but Josephine would be performing that night.

After their conversation last Monday, Mia had gone on YouTube but she'd only found some very low quality footage of Josephine singing at The Flying Pig near the university campus. All the opportunities she had missed to hear Josephine sing. But she was here now, after her first full week of work at the Pink Bean. Not only had it been a great first week, but she'd had a grand old time cracking jokes with Josephine behind the counter as well. And she'd only been late once because her bus had been stuck in traffic, which was not a common occurrence at that time of the day—about an hour before most people started on their commute. Josephine had promptly offered to pick her up in her car the next morning, seeing as she was spending a rare night in her flat in Camperdown.

Everyone she had met the past week was there. Micky and her partner Robin, whose latte should be called a wet cap—"because she's a weird American," Micky had said. Amber and Martha. Caitlin and her friend, Zoya Das, for whom Mia had to organize a farewell party at the Pink Bean in a few weeks. Kristin and Sheryl, of course. And even Lou had shown up, accompanied by the two guys from down the street whom Mia knew to be gay, so they weren't potential love interests for Lou.

Mia hadn't seen much of Lou in the past week—not as much as she would have liked anyway. Amber and Micky came in every day like clockwork, but Lou was more elusive. Mia had seen her go past the shop window a couple of times, hurrying along in her yoga gear, looking mightily busy.

Tonight, for once, Lou was not wearing a tight tank top that showed off her glorious shoulders. She was dressed in jeans and a simple t-shirt, and she looked all the more scrumptious for it. Her long hair was loose and, again, she wasn't giving Mia the time of day. Not even a nod of recognition.

Amber had offered Mia three weeks' worth of free trial lessons at Glow. The usual free trial was only one week, but Mia had promised to sit down with Micky and have a look at their online advertising. Mia had taken a course recently and Kristin had told her that her obvious marketing savvy was one of the reasons she had hired her. Mia was glad to help Amber and Micky out and she would, as soon as she was settled into her new job and got used to the new rhythm of her days. Then she would start her free trial at Glow and take a class with Lou. A full hour to ogle fair Louise from a safe distance. Far enough to remain innocuous but close enough to really get a feel for what she was like. Maybe she should go over now. Get a head start on things. Maybe exchange some pleasantries with her friends, because that was always a good way to a woman's heart. Charm the friends. Make them like you. Slowly move in from the perimeter to the center of where it's at.

Mia wasn't working tonight, but she was here to learn. She watched Kristin like a hawk as she made her way through the crowd and greeted every single patron personally, even people who had never set foot in the Pink Bean before and were only here because of Josephine's growing notoriety.

Now that Kristin was fully engaged in conversation with Caitlin and Zoya, Mia casually walked over to the table Lou and her friends were occupying.

"Hey," she said, giving them an awkward wave. "Can I get you guys something to drink?" She shot Lou a smile, hoping for at least a tiny curl upward of the lips in return, but Lou gave her the same dead-eyed stare she'd treated Mia to when they were introduced on Monday.

"I thought it was counter service," the guy without the beard said. Mia didn't know his name yet. She would need to work on remembering names more, but this week had just been an avalanche of them.

The one with the beard gave beardless guy a look, then smiled at Mia and said, "We'll take a bottle of your finest Sauvignon Blanc, please."

"Argh, we don't have our liquor license just yet, but we're working hard on it. Sorry, guys." Mia tried a furtive glance at Lou again, but she was staring in the other direction. This was beginning to feel like simply being ignored. Mia couldn't escape the vibe of animosity at this table. Beardless guy was not looking her in the eye either. "Can I get you some coffees, perhaps? Or one of the virgin cocktails we have on offer tonight?"

"We'll get it ourselves, thank you very much," beardless guy said and, with that, rose. Lou followed him so Mia was left standing there, towering over the one remaining member of their party of three.

"My name is Mia, by the way. I'm new here but we've seen each other a couple of times the past week."

"Oh, I know who you are," the guy said and ignored Mia's outstretched hand.

This was getting downright weird. What had she done to these guys?

"Okay, I'll leave you to it. Enjoy your evening," she said and skulked off in search of a warmer reception elsewhere.

## Chapter Six

"I wish they had their liquor license already," Lou said while impatiently tapping her fingers onto the counter. "I could do with a drink right about now."

"I do believe she doesn't have a clue who you are, Lou," Phil said. "Although after the way we just treated her she might start putting two and two together."

"She shouldn't be prancing around here all happy and ready to take the Pink Bean by storm. It's not right." Lou tried to calm herself down, applying the breathing techniques she had learned during her yoga training, but it wasn't working.

"Hey Phil," Amber's voice came from behind them. "How's that mermaid pose coming along?"

They both turned around. Amber always had a soothing influence on Lou and just looking into her friendly face made her feel better, a bit less alone—even though she had Phil and Jared on her side.

"There's life in this old dog's limbs yet," Phil said.

Amber introduced Phil to her partner Martha and when they discovered they were both employed in the science field

—Martha as a physics professor and Phil as a pharmaceutical researcher—they got chatting about something Lou didn't know the first thing about.

Their drinks took a long time to arrive and the queue was growing. The two people behind the counter had a hard time keeping up with the orders. Most likely because no one —not even all-foreseeing Kristin—would have expected this kind of crowd to show up for Josephine tonight. Jared had probably been right when he said this might be the last time they'd see Josephine perform at the Pink Bean. She was outgrowing the tiny venue a little more every time she took to the stage.

Both Kristin and Mia headed behind the counter to speed up the delivery of drinks and, at the sight of her only a few feet away, Lou couldn't help but flinch.

"One of these days you're going to have to tell me what you have against that girl," Amber whispered in her ear. "You two have more of a history than just having gone to the same school. Of that much I'm sure. How about you come to dinner tomorrow night? It'll just be me. Martha won't be there. We can talk. Really talk."

Lou didn't know how to say no to her boss. She also figured she would need to tell Amber at some point. Maybe then it wouldn't be so awkward when she didn't come to the Pink Bean on her breaks. "Okay." Then Lou and Phil's drinks order arrived—thankfully placed on the counter by Kristin, not Mia—and she and Phil went to find their seats again and wait for the performance to begin.

---

"The names she used to call me," Lou said. "I'm sure kids say much worse things these days, but still. It was the ferociousness of it and how it never stopped. It was like clockwork. Every single morning when I arrived at school, she would be there, with a big, evil smirk on her face and her cronies lined up next to her. There was only one way in and there was nothing I could do—not if I wanted to go to school. I felt so powerless. And she was so mean, Amber. I know it's probably hard to believe looking at her today, but by god, I have never come across anyone meaner in my life."

Amber shook her head. "If Kristin had only had a whiff of this, she would never have hired her."

"It was fifteen years ago. I honestly didn't think that seeing her again would still affect me so much. I'm sure it will get better with time, but… it's hard to be in the same room with her, because she has no idea what kind of damage she did. To her it might all have been fun and games, but for me it was hell, not only in the moment when it was happening and I was being called a *half-breed* and my father a *traitor* for marrying my mother. I was young and impressionable enough to believe I must have done something to deserve to be treated like that. That it was all my fault. It took me years to realize it had absolutely nothing to do with me. Years of painful counseling and agonizing low self-esteem."

"Do you think she has changed?" Amber asked.

Lou shrugged. "It doesn't make any difference to me whether she has or not."

Amber paused for a minute, thinking while she tapped a finger against her lips. "She must still be in her trial period. We could talk to Kristin. Tell her who her new employee really is."

Lou shook her head. "No. I don't want anyone to know, because once they do their perception of me will change as well, and I have fought so hard to become this person I am now. I wasn't always able to stand up in front of a room of people and teach. It took years of practice before I could do that."

"That's why you're such a good teacher now."

Lou ignored the compliment. Her state of mind was not one for receiving kind words well. "I just never thought I would be confronted with her again. It's such a sick twist of fate."

"This is probably not what you want to hear right now, but I strongly believe you should talk to her. Tell her who you are and who she is to you. You can't just keep this inside. And before you even have a single thought in that direction, I don't want to lose you over this. I want you to be happy at Glow, and that entails being happy with the students and your surroundings. The Pink Bean and Glow are so closely linked and, at some point, Mia might end up in one of your classes. You might not want her there. Every fiber of your being might scream *no*—which I totally understand—but I think you have no choice but to confront her."

"I can barely stand to look at her. On the outside, she doesn't seem to have changed a bit. When she tries to smile at me it makes my stomach twist up. It makes me so angry, Amber. I hardly recognize myself. That sneering grin of hers. I'm not sure I can face it."

"We can talk to her together if you like. You don't have to do this alone. You are *not* alone."

"I'll think about it." Lou drank from the tea Amber had poured. "You know when Angie and I were always fighting about something toward the end of our relationship, having children was one of our big disagreements. Some days she managed to convince me because I couldn't help but think: what if my child encounters a Mia Miller on its way? Do I really want to do that to someone?" Lou pursed her lips, trying to keep a lid on the anger surging in her heart again. "That's also what I mean when I say that the effects of cruelty are long-lasting. I want a child. I truly do. It's my one big wish. And to think that because of what Mia did to me when I was a teenager I would deny myself my most fervent wish. That's how long cruelty lives on."

"I'm so very sorry this happened to you, Lou."

The cold fist of anger wrapped around her heart meant Lou was able to keep her tears at bay. This hadn't always been the case, of course. The tears she had cried over Mia Miller. Not just over Mia, but over herself, and all the ways in which she was so obviously inadequate. She wasn't the only one getting bullied at school, even though it did feel as though Mia singled her out. In hindsight—and Lou had had a lot of that—it would have always felt that way. But the other kids seemed somehow better equipped to deal with the taunting and the being put down relentlessly. They seemed to bounce back more easily, while Lou always just wanted to slink off, wrap her arms around herself, shut out the world, and cry.

"No need for you to be sorry." Lou stared into Amber's kind green eyes.

"We need a plan." Amber scooted a little closer and put a hand on Lou's arm. "A when, where and what."

Lou tried to picture herself having the conversation with Mia that Amber was suggesting. Maybe she could do it. After all, she had a thing or two to say to her former tormentor.

"It can't be at the Pink Bean."

"No. Not in a public space. Why not talk to her at the studio? She's meant to come by to talk to Micky and me about the Google ads. Micky and I can leave so you'll have the place to yourselves."

"When is she stopping by?" Lou asked.

"We haven't set it up yet, but I can press her for it."

"Okay."

"It'll be the first thing I ask when I see her on Monday.

I'll make sure she stops by at a time when there are no more classes. Then you can talk to her in the office." The office was a room above the main studio with a large table where Micky and Amber ran Glow from their laptops. It also served as the break room.

"And then I just throw it in her face?"

"You should probably give some thought to what you're going to say. What she did to you was horrible, but it was years ago. I take it it's not revenge you're after? Because if that's the case, I'm not sure I can be part of that."

"What would you say if you were in my shoes?" Lou asked, ignoring the revenge remark.

"That's a tough one." Amber stroked her chin. "I'd try to stay calm, even though it would be very hard, but shouting has never really solved any problems, so." She gave Lou a small smile. "It's going to be tough, but maybe if you have an open conversation with her, it will change things. Not only let her know who you are and have it all out in the open, but give her a chance to say something about why she behaved so appallingly." Amber held up her hand. "Not that there exists any valid excuse for bullying, but she might want to tell you about steps she has undertaken to change. You never know."

"Because these days she's so friendly and charismatic and wrapping everyone around her finger so easily." The words came out in a tone so hard they surprised Lou.

"Didn't Micky say she thought Mia was flirting with you the other day?" Amber asked and shook her head.

"She can flirt all she wants."

Amber quirked up her eyebrows. "Some people are just so clueless."

"Thank you for inviting me over and pushing me to have this conversation. I'm not sure I'll be thanking you for the next one you're urging me to have, but this one has been good."

"I don't believe in bottling things up." Amber straightened her back. "Speaking of being very open and such," she said, making Lou wonder what would come next. "You are doing a really wonderful job at Glow. I'm so lucky to have you. I hope you're happy at my tiny studio."

"I love it." Lou expelled a small sigh of relief. "And I'm glad you feel that way."

"How about I pour us something stronger to celebrate your almost three months at Glow? No classes tomorrow, although I have been thinking about offering a Sunday class. We could alternate. If you're up for that, of course."

"No problem for me, boss." Lou was glad for the extra opportunity to work although teaching yoga never quite felt like work to her. It was her passion—and what had saved her from the spiral of negative thoughts she'd found herself in for the first part of her twenties.

## Chapter Seven

Lou didn't only not know what to do with herself, but she also didn't know where to go. Glow consisted of the room where the classes took place on the ground floor with a locker room next to it and the office on the floor above. She had opted not to be present for Amber and Micky's Google ads meeting with Mia. Not only because she didn't know the first thing about online advertising, but mainly because, even though the office was roomy and light, it felt too small and constricted for her and Mia to spend time in together.

After having paced the yoga studio a number of times and making sure the blocks and resistance bands had been stowed away carefully in the cupboard for the umpteenth time, she took herself off to the empty locker room and gazed at her reflection in the mirror.

Perhaps it was logical that Mia hadn't recognized her because she looked nothing like the frightened teenager Mia had found such great pleasure in taunting fifteen years ago. Whereas she had been gangly, skinny, and unsure what to do with the too long limbs she carried around back then, now

Lou was the kind of tall that went well with the broad shoulders garnered from doing a million downward-facing dogs and headstands. Her muscles had filled out and she moved her arms and legs with purpose.

Lou was probably the only one who could still see that gangly girl when she glanced at herself in the mirror. A girl riddled with spots on uneven, ever-oily skin, with a pair of glasses that kept sliding down her nose, and a skin color that seemed to offend so easily, so ludicrously, whereas up until she was fifteen, it had never seemed to be an issue.

"The beautiful thing about you, Lou," Angie used to say, "is that you have no idea how beautiful you are."

Back in the day, when Angie still had time for her, they would have long discussions on beauty standards and on how Lou could never perceive herself as fitting any standard, especially because for one grueling year, she had been mocked so relentlessly about how she looked.

When she glanced in the mirror she saw a woman who might have been *the most beautiful girl* Angie had ever seen, but was definitely not beautiful enough to keep Angie from choosing work over coming home at a decent time of night to clasp eyes on Lou's said beauty.

For all of those reasons, Lou didn't attach much importance to beauty. It was the most subjective thing, anyway. Back in school, everyone thought Mia was the most beautiful girl in their year, but Lou knew how ugly she really was. And sure, Jared had described Mia as hot, and maybe to him she was—because he had entirely different standards for beauty than Lou had—but Lou was sure Mia ceased to be anything remotely related to beautiful after she had told Jared about their history.

"There you are." Amber's voice came from behind her. "I've asked Mia to stay behind for a minute. Told her you had something to ask her. She's upstairs. Micky and I are just packing up and will be out of your hair in five minutes." Amber came to stand next to her and looked at her in the reflection in the mirror. "If you need to come see me afterwards, I'll be home." She put a gentle hand on Lou's shoulder. "Remember, you are not alone."

"Thanks." Lou took a deep breath, wondering what stories Mia was making up in her head right now about why Lou had asked her to stay. Maybe she believed her feeble attempts at flirting had worked. Or that Lou wanted to apologize for giving her the cold shoulder at the open mic last Friday. Or perhaps she did have a clue. Perhaps she did know. Either way, the time to stop guessing had come. "I'll be in touch later," Lou said and watched Amber leave. They had agreed not to tell Micky—the fewer who people knew, the better. So when Micky walked past Lou on her way out, she surely had very different ideas about the conversation that was about to occur, and shot Lou a big fat wink, accompanied by a heartfelt, "Have fun."

———

Mia was sitting in Amber's chair, but had swiveled it around so she was looking out the window.

"Hey," she said when Lou walked in.

Lou didn't close the door, afraid it might have a too suffocating effect on her.

"Thanks for staying," she said, trying to keep her voice from shaking.

"You've got me intrigued." Mia painted on one of her crooked grins. When she smiled, everything about her lit up — which Lou thought an infuriating quality. "I was convinced you didn't like me very much."

Lou tried to remember Amber's words and remain calm. She sat down in Micky's chair, leaving a good distance between them. When she tried to speak the first time, the words died in the back of her throat. She had to swallow hard and try again. "You really have no idea who I am?"

Mia narrowed her eyes. "Of course I do. You're Louise, known as Lou by everyone around here, and you teach yoga in this very studio." She tilted her head. "What am I missing?"

Lou took another deep breath, then finally said the words. "I'm Louise Hamilton of the graduating class of 2003 at Queen Mary's College For Girls." Lou willed herself to study Mia's face. To observe what happened to it when the penny dropped.

"We went to the same school?" Mia asked innocently. "I really hadn't recognized you. Were we in the same class?"

Lou had to deploy every single tactic she had ever learned in yoga and meditation training to stay calm and not lash out and start shouting. All she did was shake her head and say, as evenly as possible, "I'm the *half-breed* you and your gang waited for just behind the gate every single morning. The girl you thought so little of, you didn't think twice about calling her names and insulting her on a daily basis. The girl who made you feel superior and feared by everyone else. Your so-called friends included."

"What?" Mia's face was starting to sink. "No."

"Oh, yes."

Mia's shoulders slumped and she looked away. She said something but because her face was turned away and she mumbled it so quietly, Lou couldn't understand.

"I didn't quite hear that," Lou said.

Mia turned to her, her knee bopping up and down. "That was a long time ago," she murmured.

"I remember every minute of it."

Mia glanced at her, then quickly averted her gaze again, looking at her hands which she had gathered in her lap. She seemed to have shrunk a few centimeters and there was nothing left of the self-confidence she carried herself with around the Pink Bean—and which had annoyed Lou greatly.

"I'm so, so sorry," Mia said. "I—I don't know what else to say."

"There's nothing you can say. You did your damage a long time ago, that much is true, and nothing can change that now."

"Have you, er, told anyone?" Mia asked.

"Amber knows. She's the only one."

"And those two guys you came to the Pink Bean with? The ones who treated me like dirt," Mia said. It wasn't a question. She was putting the pieces together in her head.

Lou nodded.

"Are you going to tell Kristin? Is that what this is about?" She cleared her throat. "I would understand if you wanted some sort of payback. If you would want to get me fired." A tear trickled down Mia's cheek.

"I don't want revenge," Lou managed to say. "I just wanted you to know who I was and remember what you did." As she had done quite a few times over the weekend, she pondered again whether it would give her any kind of pleasure to inform Kristin about who Mia really was. But Lou knew it wouldn't. This wasn't about any sort of revenge. The tears that ran down Mia's face in ever bigger streams didn't give her the least bit of pleasure. This was the kind of situation in which not an ounce of pleasure could ever be derived. "Because it seemed to me like you had chosen to forget all about your former ways and present yourself like an entirely different person."

"That's because I am." It came out as more of a howl than a string of words. "I am not that person anymore. I loathe the girl I was then. I'm ashamed of her—of myself."

"As you should be."

Mia shook her head while wiping some tears off her face. "I'm so sorry. Is there anything I can do? I'll do anything."

"There is no penance for your crimes. There is no absolution." The tone of her own voice was beginning to scare Lou again. "You're just going to have to live with what you did for the rest of your life. What you did to me and the others. Reduced us to toys for your cruel, cruel games. I cried myself to sleep for a long time after I left Queen Mary, just because of you. Because you existed and our paths crossed and you were so fucked-up you could only express it by being mean. It took me a long time to realize that it was not me who was the screwed-up one, the one who deserved to be called names like that, but it was you. The kind of person you must have been to have to resort to that sort of brutality every single day. A vain narcissist who got off on other people's tears. A control freak who couldn't stand the slightest word of criticism aimed at herself. In fact, I feel sorry for you, Mia. I hated you for a very long time, but now, I feel genuinely sorry for you. The kinds of fucked-up you must be."

"What do you want me to do?" Mia seemed to be gaining back a bit of her composure. "Do you want me to leave the Pink Bean?"

"I'm not here to blackmail you. I'm just here to remind you. And to finally say what I've wanted to say to you forever. And I will remind you of who you truly are every single day, you can be sure of that. There will be no more carefree prancing about the Pink Bean when I'm around, or when Amber is around. I will always have my eye on you, because I want you to remember." This was starting to sound a lot like the revenge Lou had said she didn't want.

"This may mean nothing to you, but I *have* changed. That angry young girl has nothing to do with who I am now. I'm so sorry for what I put you through. I really am."

"I don't care who you are today. You could be volunteering at a homeless shelter and feed stray cats and participate in anti-bullying programs every single day for the rest of your life. In my eyes, you will never be redeemed. Because I don't believe that sort of inborn cruelty can ever leave a person."

"It's your prerogative to believe that. I won't try to change your mind. I will keep my distance from you."

"And you won't come to any of my yoga classes."

Mia nodded. "I'm sorry," she said again. "If it's all right with you, I would like to go now."

"Go." Lou watched Mia as she tried to gather herself and stood up, steadying herself against the table. She watched her walk out of the door and waited for a sense of relief to set in, for her own limbs to relax and a weight to drop off her shoulders, but none of that happened. Instead, she started shaking uncontrollably and burst into tears.

## Chapter Eight

The one thought Mia couldn't get out of her head was that the woman who had just decimated her, confronted her with all the wrongdoings of her youth, was really Louise Hamilton. Spindly Lou with the long arms and legs that always remained motionless whenever Mia unleashed one of her vile attacks on the girl. And they had been vile and vicious and as much a cry for help as any of the other things Mia got up to back then, but no help ever came.

She felt deeply ashamed, but more than that she felt flabbergasted, taken aback by the harshness of Lou's words. A harshness she surely deserved, still now. Just as much as Mia turning up in the Pink Bean must have felt like Lou's past coming back to haunt her, it felt like that to Mia now. A past she had long forgotten, even though snatches of it turned up unbidden in nightmares in the middle of the night when she woke up in a sweat and didn't know what to do with herself because of the shame that engulfed her.

Was she still that narcissist Lou had described earlier?

Was she still, underneath the veneer of good cheer and will, so cruel?

*No, no, no.* As she made her way to the bus stop, and realized she'd just missed one and had to wait twenty minutes for the next one, Mia told herself no. She was no longer any of these things, had perhaps never been them. Not that there were any excuses for how she had behaved, but she, too, had had to expel a few demons from her life to get where she was now. Or, put more accurately, her mother had to leave her father before life got any better for Mia.

Mia could kick herself for not recognizing Lou, but she looked so different. She had confidence now, not the brazen kind, but the subtle kind of confidence that comes from true self-acceptance. Not the overbearing kind Mia tried to display in her teens, when she was just as insecure as the next girl in her year. But she had inherited a brazenness from her father. The 'gift' to shoot down any critic before they could even open their mouth.

How could she ever make this up to Lou? And to think that before Lou had treated her so cold-heartedly last Friday she had entertained the notion of asking her out.

Mia paced around the bus shelter, trying to come up with some sort of action that could adequately convey how sorry she was for what she had done, for the person she used to be. Then it hit her that Amber also knew. Amber, who had just invited her into her office and asked her a bunch of questions about online advertising and had acted as if Mia was doing her a big favor. Amber, who would now always see the girl her employee, Lou, had described to her instead of the woman Mia was now.

Mia had felt so good after her first week in the Pink Bean. A few days later, there was nothing left of that ecstatic feeling that comes with finding a job that really suits you and working with the kind of people who make you feel like you've found a new home as well as a place of work.

And it was all her own damn fault. Nothing would be the same again now. Maybe she should quit and start over somewhere else. Or get the plans for the Newtown branch rolling as quickly as possible. Only Amber knew—and Lou, of course. Would that be a tenable situation? There was only one way to find out. By going to the Pink Bean every morning and facing the music. After all, that's what she had made Lou live through every morning when they were seventeen.

Mia inhaled deeply. If the slabs of the sidewalk would be so kind as to open up right then and swallow her whole, Mia would gladly sink under the ground and never set foot above again. She was guilty. She had done all the things Lou had said she'd done. She was a bully. Had been a bully. But the adage *once a bully, always a bully* didn't hold up. Not for her. Mia flinched whenever someone raised their voice impertinently at someone else. She always spoke up if she noticed someone was being treated unfairly, because she couldn't bear someone lording power they didn't have over another person. She couldn't stand inequality—one of the reasons she loved the Pink Bean so much—and disagreed with everything her father had taught her when she was a child. Not that she saw her father anymore. That chapter of her life had been closed a long time ago.

Her bus finally arrived and she got on, finding a spot at the back the way she always did. It had started to drizzle and she looked out over the wet Sydney streets and the way the lights of the traffic and billboards reflected in the small puddles left everywhere. At one point, she'd contemplated leaving, getting a fresh start somewhere else, in another country, where she would never run into anyone from her past, would never need to be confronted with it ever again, until she realized that hoping for no confrontation, for no comeuppance was ridiculous, because all those feelings lay within her. She would always see herself when she looked into the mirror, no matter how much she had changed and tried to do right by others, tried to make up with good deeds for the bad ones she had committed, as if it was a simple credit-debit balance that needed to be evened out. She would always be the person who had said and done those things—and now Louise Hamilton had turned up to remind her of that.

What did she think anyway? That she could progress through her life without ever meeting any of the girls she had called the most ghastly things? Mia had always known that life was not that kind of fairytale, and now she had the proof. She would find a way to deal with Louise, with that side of her past, of herself, and live with it in a more aware way than she had been doing. It was the only way.

---

"Is everything all right?" Jo asked. "You seem a bit flighty today. And if you look at that door one more time, I'm afraid it might come off its hinges just from the sheer intensity of your stare."

Mia was dreading the moment Amber and Lou would walk in. And she was sure she looked a lot worse for wear. She hadn't slept a wink, kept tossing and turning in bed, trying to come up with ways to make things better. Things were already better for Lou—how could they not be?—but if she couldn't make things better, then she wanted to make up for the time Lou had lost because of her. For the hours she spent crying because of Mia, hours of her life she would never get back.

"Rough night," Mia said.

"Hot date? And is she about to walk in?" Jo joked.

"If only," Mia said. She could not confide in Jo. After leaving Queen Mary, she had never told anyone about what she had done. She had started fresh, gone to university. She lived at home her freshman year until her father had been removed from her family's daily life. She was never going to let her mother live alone with that man. Then she'd moved to Newtown and had fallen in love with it.

Nobody she had gotten to know after high school knew the first thing about the vile acts she was capable of. Nobody must know. Mia had rebuilt herself one day at a time, had distanced herself from the influence of her father and the girl she had allowed herself to become a little bit more every day as time progressed. And now there she was fifteen years later. Perfectly capable of not thinking about her past for days on end. Until now. It had come back as hard and sudden as a slap in the face.

"Come on, Mia. A girl like you. The admirers must be lining up," Jo said.

Mia huffed out a laugh. "No one is doing any such thing."

"What about Lou? Do you still have the hots for her?" Jo pursed her lips together.

The sound of Lou's name shot another jolt of shame through her. Mia shook her head. "No. That's never going to happen."

"Why not? What happened?"

Mia feverishly wished someone would come into the café right about now. She wouldn't even mind if it was one of Lou's friends who would pretend she didn't exist. But the door remained closed and the customers who were present seemed perfectly content nursing their coffees.

"Nothing." Damn it. Mia had clearly said too much already.

"Did you make a move on her at the open mic night?" Josephine didn't let up.

Mia shook her head. "Nothing like that."

"Because Caitlin and I were talking the other day and, provided that Lou bats for our team, the two of you would make a pretty stunning couple."

"What? No." Mia had to keep herself from raising her voice.

"Okay, okay. I get it. You're not interested, but I sure thought you were for a minute there," Jo said.

Finally, the door opened and someone walked in. Before Mia could get a look at the new patrons, her heart skipped a beat. But it wasn't Lou. It was a woman whom she had seen at the Pink Bean almost every day and who had flashed her a few smiles that could hardly be misunderstood.

"Hi Daisy," Jo said. "I'll let Mia take care of you today."

Hackles fully up, Mia served Daisy her coffee, reacting as neutrally as possible to her mild flirtations.

"Okay, if it's going to be like this whenever it's your time of the month, you're going to have to be very honest with me," Josephine said. "You nearly stared poor Daisy out of here with that ominous glare of yours, and we both know she has the hots for you."

"I'm sorry. I'm having a massive off day. I don't feel much like flirting or talking for that matter."

"Hey, we all have them. No need to explain yourself to me. Just a heads-up, that's all I ask."

Mia had to laugh at Jo's earnest face, but she couldn't say anything else. She had made her own bed years ago, and she would have to lie in it alone.

"Feel free to take your break." Jo actually put a hand on her shoulder. "I'll even pour you some coffee and bring it over to you. Put your feet up for a bit."

"Thanks, Jo. I'm fine. I'm a woman. I can take it."

"Hear, hear," Jo said, and poured Mia a cup of coffee anyway.

Whilst they were chatting, Mia had missed Amber and Lou approaching. Then they stood in front of her.

"I've got it," Jo said. "Mia is feeling a little off today. Feel free to sit with Amber and Lou if you like," she said to Mia. "Take a load off."

Lou and Amber didn't say anything, so Mia quickly said, "That's fine. I don't need a break."

"What's up with them?" Jo asked after she had brought Lou and Amber their beverages. "Have you all synced your cycles already?" She went quiet for a few seconds while she wiped the counter. "Did something happen last night when you went to Glow to help Amber and Micky out?"

Mia wasn't sure if she would be able to keep her relationship to Lou a secret from Josephine, after all. The woman was too damn observant. Spending four and a half hours together crammed behind a coffee shop counter will do that to you. She would need to say something just to get Jo off her back. But she didn't know Jo all that well yet. They'd met barely a week ago. She would need to be firm and vague at the same time.

"Look, Jo, something did happen, but it's not something any one of us is going to talk about, so I'm going to need you to give it a rest."

Jo draped her dish towel over the sink, then turned to Mia. "This is the Pink Bean. You can try to keep a secret, but from my years of experience in this place, I can tell you it's probably not going to work."

"I'm sorry, but I really can't tell you more. And I would appreciate it if you didn't quiz Lou and Amber about it. Just leave it be."

"Okay." Jo nodded. "That bad, huh?"

Mia contemplated asking Kristin if they could start the

hiring process for a morning barista sooner, so she wouldn't have to do the morning shifts anymore. Then she thought about giving her notice again. She'd be out of a job, but would that really be so bad compared to having to walk on eggshells around here every single day? She'd only been here a couple of hours this morning and already it was proving so hard.

"Please excuse me for a second." Mia headed into the bathroom and stood inside the stall for long, silent minutes. Apart from the anguish in her own head before, during and after she was doing the actual bullying, Mia had never been properly punished for what she had done. Maybe that time had now finally come.

## Chapter Nine

After her confrontation with Mia, Lou felt different. Lighter on her feet. Like a weight had—finally—been lifted. And yes, she still cringed every time she ran into Mia at the Pink Bean, but at least she didn't have to fear that Mia would join her yoga class and the dread of Mia confronting *her* had been lifted.

Amber had been right—she usually was. Getting it all out into the open had been so much better than carrying it around in agonizing silence. Lou should have known better. Her yoga training should have guided her in the same direction that Amber had sent her in, but when it came to such deeply personal matters, training tended to fail the individual.

Now she sat, enjoying the wine that was being poured generously, and the laughter and easy conversation of these four women she had gotten to know over the past few months since she'd joined the staff of Glow.

Robin and Martha had tried to be supportive of their respective partners and had come to a few yoga classes.

Before Lou had become an instructor at Glow, she had actually been in one of the classes Martha and Robin had attended together. Their disrespectful giggling had got on Lou's nerves and their yoga habit had not stuck.

"I used to believe otherwise, but not everyone can be converted," Amber had said laconically.

Amber's partner Martha had cooked a vegan meal at her home in Camperdown, and Lou had carpooled with Micky and Robin. Working at Glow felt like an automatic inclusion in their group, which often extended to Kristin and Sheryl and occasionally to Caitlin and Josephine.

Lou had lived in Brisbane for almost ten years and although she had returned to Sydney frequently, most of the close friendships she had enjoyed before leaving had petered out. Besides, Lou was a different person now. It had been easy enough to rekindle her friendship with Phil, who now was a dad and a husband, but other relationships hadn't fared so well.

Lives can diverge, time changes people and Lou wasn't the best at keeping in touch and keeping the fires of long-distance friendships stoked. She had also learned that knowing someone in your early twenties is very different to knowing someone in your early thirties. So she was glad to have found this group of almost friends that came with the job.

"Can you believe I've never been to Brisbane," Robin said. "Is it something that can't be missed?"

"Brisbane is lovely. It's much… gentler than Sydney. Much smaller, of course, which suited me fine. And a whole lot cheaper as well. So yes, you should go."

"Was it hard coming back to Sydney?" Martha asked.

"Yes and no." Lou looked into her pale eyes. When she first met Amber, she would never have pictured someone like Martha as her partner, even though she couldn't quite explain why. "My family is here and we've always been very close, so it's been great to be back. Although living with my parents again took some getting used to. But sure, it was hard to leave the city where I'd made a life. I just really needed a change. And to not run into my ex, because that's what happens in Brisbane. You run into the people you don't want to run into all the time." She scoffed. "Sydney is a new start for me. Well, perhaps not really new anymore as I've been back for six months now. But I grew up in this city so it's good to be back. To come home."

Martha nodded and just gave a prolonged *hmm* as an answer.

"What?" Lou asked. "Why are you looking at me like that?"

"I don't know… You're such a gentle soul. You have the same glow about you that Amber has. What kind of madwoman in Brisbane let go of you?"

"Stop flirting with my colleague, babe," Amber said. "I'm sitting right here."

"I'm not flirting." Martha gazed at Amber and stared into her eyes. "Why would I flirt with anyone else when I'm with you?" She turned her attention back to Lou. "I'm just observing."

"Lou, please don't feel as though you need to talk about your ex just because Martha is overly curious."

Lou appreciated how protective Amber was about her, and had become even more so since she'd told her about Mia. She had all the qualities of an excellent mentor. "It's okay. I don't mind." Lou took a sip from her wine, then continued. "To put it quite simply, Angie and I grew apart. About three years ago she got this new job and it started taking up more and more of her time. Other things became important to her, like making more money and going to the right kind of networking events. Things that had never interested her—or me—before. But most of all, she was never home anymore. She was always at some after-work cocktail party schmoozing with her bosses or at some self-improvement seminar over the weekend. In a nutshell, we never really recovered from that."

"Did she do CrossFit?" Micky asked. "A-type personalities prefer those kind of brutal workouts to the more holistic and gentler benefits yoga has to offer."

"I'll have you know that people with lots of different personalities do CrossFit," Robin replied.

"But not a lot of them have time for yoga in their schedule," Micky said, sending Robin a wide smile.

"Every time," Robin said. "Do yoga and CrossFit really need to be pitted against each other every single time? Besides, Lou wasn't finished with her story yet. You work with her and get to ask her questions all day long, but I don't." Robin blew Micky a kiss and refocused her attention on Lou. "I'm very sorry for the rude interruption. I would try to make some excuse for my worse half's behavior but you must know her well by now." Robin winked at Lou.

Micky hadn't been too far off in her observation. Robin did remind her of Angie in some ways, but as far as Lou knew, only the good parts of their personalities matched.

"That's about all that there was to it in the end. Well, apart from the fact that my biological clock started ticking and Angie was becoming more and more of an expert in ignoring that. I'll be thirty-two soon. I have some time, but not that much either."

"You want children?" Martha asked.

"Yes. I do. Very much so."

"Well you have the womb, all you need is some seed. I can always ask my ex-husband Darren. He produces marvelous children and he seems to still be very fertile." Micky shook her head.

Lou remembered the day not so long ago when Micky had arrived at Glow very upset because she had just heard that the father of her teenage children was going to become a dad again.

"Men are just such clichés," Micky continued. "First he trades me in for a younger model, then he gets said younger model pregnant. Can it be any more by the book?"

"That wasn't quite how things went down," Amber said in her steady, but stern voice.

"Oh, I know. But I'm allowed to be a little upset about this. Chris and Liv are going to have a baby brother or sister, for crying out loud. That was never the plan."

"So many things never go according to plan," Martha said. "I believe they call that life."

"That's right," Robin said. "Did you ever plan that you would be sitting here with someone like me, my darling?" She blew Micky another kiss.

"That obnoxious sweaty woman ordering wet cappuccinos every day." Micky shook her head while a big smile appeared on her face. "Not in a million years."

"Nor had I planned to still be in Australia at this point, but look at me, tied to my woman and her country," Robin said.

The only slightly difficult bit about hanging out with these four, Lou thought, was that they were all so happily coupled up. For someone still in the aftermath of a break-up, it was sometimes hard to face these displays of love. These displays of what Lou could have had if, perhaps, she'd fought harder for her relationship.

But she and Angie needed to have been fighting together to win that particular fight. All the while Lou was trying her best to bridge the gap that had formed between her and Angie, she never got the impression Angie was in the trenches with her, battling for their survival. Whereas now that Lou had been gone from Brisbane for six months, Angie seemed to be regretting her unwillingness to fight when it mattered most. But it was too late. Angie was part of her past now. Lou had to look to the future.

"Do you have a plan?" Martha asked Lou. "To conceive and all of that. I presume you won't be going about it the all-natural way."

"Hardly." Lou shook her head. "Ideally, I would find a new partner first so that I won't be a single mother, even though that doesn't solve the seed problem, of course." She chuckled. "Then I figured we'd go to a sperm bank. That's about as much of a plan as I have at this point." Although the need to have children was very concrete to Lou, she felt like she couldn't fine-tune the details until she had first fully gotten over Angie and, perhaps, explored the possibility of a new relationship.

"That's a long road to go down," Martha said, "but it'll be worth every step of the way. Having children is just… how to say this… what makes you simultaneously the strongest and the most vulnerable. Definitely life-changing. Nothing will ever be the same again. And it will be hard, but it will also be worth every single second."

"I second that. My children are teenagers, so there are a lot of hard times in our house right now," Micky said.

"Sounds to me like we need to find Lou a girlfriend," Robin said. "Or do you have your sights set on anyone in particular already?"

"God no. I've basically just been licking my wounds after Angie." She sank her teeth into her bottom lip. "I recently installed Tinder, but I haven't had many reasons to swipe right. Besides, it's such a superficial way to meet someone, solely based on looks, while looks are really not that important to me. Not to say that they are of no value at all, but other things are more important. Things you can't see on your phone screen in a matter of seconds."

"There must be a few single lesbians in your yoga classes," Martha said. "Or has the boss forbidden you to woo your students?"

"I would never sleep with a student. I find it unethical," Lou said. "Amber and I are fully on the same page when it comes to that."

"I don't remember ever telling you it's unethical," Amber said.

"Oh, how our yogi has softened of late," Micky said. "It's obviously Martha's good influence." Micky turned to Lou. "Amber used to think exactly like you. No matter how many times I argued that there was nothing unethical about saying yes when a student asks you out."

"It's different when they ask you out," Amber said.

"Oh yeah? How many times did you get asked out and how many times did you say yes?" Micky asked.

"That's beside the point." Amber stared Lou in the eye. "Just to be clear. If anyone asks you out after a class, feel free to say yes. I know you would never take advantage of your position as a teacher."

"Maybe I should come to one of your classes, after all," Robin said. "Just to keep an eye on who's ogling you."

"That would be the day," Micky said.

"Or…" Robin continued. "Why don't we have a go at Tinder together right now? Surely the five of us will be a better judge of character based on someone's looks than just you." She sat there snickering. Micky was driving tonight, a fact of which Robin had taken eager advantage.

But Micky didn't come to Lou's rescue, neither did Amber or Martha. Maybe they were curious about the sort of people one could encounter via a phone app, or they were so invested in Lou's plight to find someone—even though

Lou wasn't all that invested in it herself—they'd had enough of being rational at this late hour on a Saturday night.

"Do you have your phone on you?" Robin asked.

"Yes." Lou was already reaching for it in her bag which hung from her chair. No harm could be done with this exercise. It was just a bit of fun really. "Here you go." Lou unlocked her phone, opened the Tinder app, and handed it to Robin, the self-appointed ringleader in the quest to find Lou a girlfriend.

"How does this work?" Martha asked. "I'm too old to be up to speed with these things."

"It's easy," Robin said. "First you create your profile and configure what you're looking for, which I assume Lou has already done. Then you get to see an array of profile pictures and you swipe right on the ones you like and left on the ones you don't like."

"And this is for lesbians?" Martha asked, an incredulous note to her voice. "I find that very hard to believe. It's too judgmental."

"What? You think lesbians can't be judgmental bitches?" Robin said. She certainly was the life of the party tonight.

"I'm so proud of you, babe," Micky said. "And all the words of wisdom you have for everyone tonight." She brought a hand to Robin's neck and kept it there.

"It's not exclusively for lesbians. Anyone can register, then you just set a preference for whether you're searching for men or women," Lou said.

"Which often means you have to go through a lot of fake profiles put up by men stupid enough to believe that's a great way to bed lesbians," Robin said.

"You seem to know an awful lot about Tinder, babe," Micky said. "Should I be worried?"

"Of course not, my love," Robin said in an exaggerated sweet tone. "But I recently helped Meredith set up a profile.

She's actually been on a few dates already." She looked as if a lightbulb had just gone off in her head. "Speaking of Meredith…" Robin fixed her gaze on Micky, then on Lou. "We'll probably encounter her on here, so I can save you the trouble of swiping if you like, and make something happen."

"No, no, no," Micky said. "Meredith is not for Lou. She's a stockbroker, for heaven's sake. And a CrossFitter like you. She hasn't set foot in a yoga studio in her life."

"So? Opposites can attract?" Robin said.

"Do your swiping already," Micky said. "If we happen to come across Meredith, Lou can decide based on what she looks like."

"Okay, here we go. Everyone huddle around," Robin said.

As Lou made her way behind Robin's chair, so did Micky, Martha and Amber, and she thought about the strange turn the night had taken. But no matter how strange, she was also touched by the interest in her love life—and ultimately her happiness—these four women had taken. Although she was well aware this whole Tinder thing was also just very entertaining for them.

Robin started swiping and the first ten profiles they encountered were either met with a resounding *No* from everyone or a *fake lesbian* from Robin, the expert.

"See," Robin said then. "I told you."

"That's Meredith," Micky said. "Left or right, Lou?"

"Just so you know, she does have a softer side and likes to recite poetry at the Pink Bean open mic nights," Amber said.

"How's her poetry?" Lou asked.

"Does it really matter?" Micky asked, agitation in her voice. She was getting very worked up over this.

Lou peered at the screen. Meredith had adopted the typical selfie-pose for her profile picture. It was taken from above to make her face look as skinny as possible and her lips were not exactly drawn into a smile, but more into what was meant to be a seductive sort of pout.

"How old is she?" Lou asked, figuring she could ask that sort of discerning question in the company she was in this evening.

"Thirty-six," Robin said.

Lou scanned the face looking back at her some more. Clear brown eyes. A few freckles gathered around a small nose. Short hair mussed about to look perfectly imperfect.

"Okay, swipe right."

"Yessss," Robin said and swiped.

"What happens next?" Martha asked.

"Depending on whether Meredith swipes right on Lou, they can then message each other." Robin gave Lou an appreciative once-over. "There is no way anyone on this app, and certainly not Meredith, will swipe left on you. I don't mean to objectify your looks, Lou, but you're as drop-dead gorgeous as they come."

Lou had had enough drinks to laugh away Robin's comment.

"Anyway, now that we're starting to find our groove, let's continue," Robin said. She sounded as though she had just won a small amount at the slot machine and was now gunning for the big jackpot, confident that she would get it, no matter that the house always wins.

They all said *No* in unison a few more times, debated a few others, which Lou vetoed as left swipes in the end, until another familiar face popped up.

"Ooh, interesting," Robin said. "I hadn't figured Mia to be single and certainly not as someone looking for love on a dating app."

"Swipe left," Amber said, her tone firm.

Robin glanced at her. "Why?"

"Just do it, Robin," Amber said.

"Are you sure, Lou? You and Mia are the two hot young singles of our group now and, truth be told, you'd make a cute couple. There's something about her, don't you think?"

That was the second time this week someone had said Lou and Mia would make a good couple. It just went to show how deceiving appearances could be. Which made Lou decide it was time to put an end to this whole Tinder business.

"That's a definite left," she said to Robin. "And I think I've had about enough now."

"Okay. You're in charge," Robin said.

"Are you sure, babe?" Micky said. "You seemed to be getting a little carried away there."

Robin handed the phone back to Lou. "I was quite disappointed with what was on offer to be honest. Which makes me realize I'm doubly lucky to have already found you." She leaned over and kissed Micky on the mouth.

"Maybe Tinder is not the way to true love, despite its many amazing features," Martha said sarcastically.

Then Lou's phone beeped. She hadn't closed the Tinder app yet and a notification came in that Meredith had swiped right on her profile as well. She showed the screen to Robin.

"It could work, you know," Robin said. "Stranger things have happened."

"I'll message her tomorrow then," Lou said. "First I need to know how I'll feel about this after a good night's sleep." She put away her phone, still a bit perturbed by seeing Mia's face out of the blue again, but grateful that Robin was too tipsy to inquire about it further, although Lou had seen Micky furrow her brow at her and Amber's adamant *no*.

"Keep me posted. Just so I know what to say to Meredith on Monday," Robin said. "Just for the record, she is a Cross-Fitting stockbroker, but impossible as it may seem, she has a heart of gold. A heart that's been trampled on one too many times."

"Hence the poetry, I presume," Martha said drily.

Amber and Micky burst out laughing, while Lou wondered whether she'd be going on a date some time soon.

## Chapter Ten

On Sunday morning Mia went about her regular slow wake up routine. A lot slower than before she had started working at the Pink Bean, although the annoying side-effect of having to set her alarm for five o'clock on weekdays was that her body woke up of its own accord at the same time on Sunday.

She took the Saturday edition of *The Sydney Morning Herald*—she preferred the feel of old-fashioned paper in her hands at the weekend over her tablet screen—and went to her favorite brunch spot around the corner from her small flat off King Street.

After she ordered and sat down, she realized, just like she had done the Sunday before, that soon she would be opening up an establishment that would be direct competition with this place where she'd had many a good breakfast and spent many a lovely hour perusing the newspaper or watching the world go by. But this was Newtown, and another coffee shop had just closed at the other end of this busy boulevard, and such, also, was life.

The Larder was right next to her favorite independent

cinema and, as she always did on Sunday morning, she studied the movie review section, compared it to what was on offer next door, and then bought a ticket for the afternoon showing at three. This allowed her ample time to stop by to see Annie, who ran a women's bookshop across the street, and who more often than not knew exactly what to recommend according to Mia's tastes.

Fueled by her big breakfast, and the damn good coffee they served at The Larder, Mia headed to the bookshop with a spring in her step. It had been an eventful week, one that had taken its toll on her sleep and her peace of mind, but on Sunday one had no choice but to let it all go and relax. She was in her own neighborhood, which, for now, had no Pink Bean affiliation yet. This was where she felt good, strutting along King Street, nodding at Sue from the juice bar and Ahmed who was opening up his kebab shop. The people she had known for years and who made up the backdrop of her life. It was in Newtown that she had become someone else, that she had freed herself from the shackles of her old behavior, from the relentless soundtrack of her father's words in her ear. From the girl she once was. A girl who had deserved to be loathed for sure, but she had been that girl and as disgusting as her behavior had been—cocky, cruel and trying to impress the wrong people—at some point between then and now, Mia had found it inside herself to forgive. If she couldn't forgive herself for her past mistakes, what point was there in going on? Forgiving didn't mean forgetting. She would always remember, but only she knew how lost she had been at the time, how lonely a teenager with a dozen friends can actually be.

Mia stopped in front of the bookshop window and checked to see what had changed. There was one new book on display, but all the rest had remained the same. The bell dinged as she went inside and Annie, forever positioned on a high stool behind the counter, gave her a wave. Most times she came here, Mia was the only patron in the shop, and it was no different this Sunday. Other people would sometimes come in, but just browse the books—sometimes even being so bold as to take a picture of a cover with their phone so they could get the book online later—and never buy anything.

Mia went up to the counter. "What have you got for me today, Annie?"

Annie's face lit up at Mia's question. "Are you in the mood for something old or something new?"

Mia pretended to think about this, even though Annie asked her the same question every time. "Old, of course," Mia replied.

"There are so many good new books out, Mia, you really have to start on them sooner rather than later, especially..." Annie paused.

"Especially what?"

Annie's face darkened. "I got another offer on the shop. I'm not sure I can still afford to refuse this one."

"Pages?" Mia asked.

Annie nodded. "And guess what the kicker is. They don't want to turn it into just another Pages branch. They want to make it look like an actual independent bookshop, even though it won't be, of course. They want to fool the customer because, according to them, the customer wants to be fooled."

Mia shook her head. "What an utter disgrace."

"They've even offered me an"—she curled her fingers into air quotes—"'advisory position'. But you know me, Mia. You've been coming here for years. Even though their prime business is books, I can't work for a big corporation like Pages. I've had this shop for almost twenty years. I've had no bosses and no upper management to report to. I've had control over what goes on the shelves and what doesn't—nothing by Jeremy Clarkson, for instance. There's just no way I will let some marketing department populated by twenty-somethings tell me what to put on the shelves of *my* bookshop. They probably don't know their Jane Austen from their Charlotte Brontë." Annie held up a copy of *Wuthering Heights*. "This, for example, is no Jane Austen." Her voice broke a fraction, then she shrugged. "Oh well, I guess I'm ready for retirement, anyway."

"You're in the prime of your life, Annie." Mia accepted the copy of *Wuthering Heights* Annie handed her. She glanced around the shop. Because Annie had owned it for as long as the shop had been open, it was a big space that had survived the trend of ever-smaller store spaces. She and her partner lived in the flat above. Annie's entire life revolved around this shop.

Annie scoffed. "Hardly," she said. "*You* are in the prime of your life. So let's quickly change the subject. I don't want to depress my most loyal customer with sad tales of my gloomy fate." She gave Mia a crooked smile. "Have you found a girlfriend yet?"

Mia knew it was meant in jest, and that Annie, who was as sweet as they came, mostly asked the question out of habit. But today Mia didn't feel like giving her usual answer. Instead she said, "You know these days it's not every person in their twenties and thirties' biggest dream to find a partner, have 2.4 babies and move to a house in the suburbs. Being single is a perfectly valid way to live your life, despite what the general perception of us might be."

"Oh, I'm sure. I guess I'm just old-fashioned that way," Annie said, then their attention was snagged by the bell chiming. Instinctively, they both stared at the door. Mia's heart did a double take when she recognized Lou. So much for a relaxing Sunday. She took a deep breath. She'd finish her purchase and head to the cinema early, have a stiff drink on the terrace in front. All thoughts of the possibility of Annie's bookshop ceasing to exist were pushed to the back of her mind. These days, when faced with Lou—who now could only represent the mistakes Mia had made in the past—she had to go into survival mode.

Seeing as Mia was the only other customer in the shop, Lou had looked her straight in the eye. She'd given no sign of recognition as far as Mia could tell.

"Are you all right, Mia?" Annie asked. "You look like you've seen a ghost."

"I'm fine. Can I pay for this, please? I need to get going."

"So quickly?"

Mia nervously shuffled her weight from one foot to the other. "Yes. Sorry." Taking that deep breath hadn't helped one bit. God, she really needed to push Kristin to get moving on the new Pink Bean plans. Find a suitable space. In fact, instead of going to the theatre early, Mia would walk along King Street with wide open eyes and search for suitable spaces herself. The sooner they found one, the sooner she could stay away from the Darlinghurst branch and avoid Lou altogether, because this was starting to do her head in.

"Is it because of Louise? You've been jumpy ever since she walked in."

"You know her?"

"Yes. Her mother and I have been volunteers at the same soup kitchen since we were in our twenties. I've known Louise since she was a little girl."

The mention of Lou as a little girl felt like another blow to Mia's stomach.

"I take it you know her as well and things didn't end well?" Annie waggled her eyebrows in quick succession a few times.

Mia shook her head. "I really need to go now. I'll see you next week."

"As you wish," Annie said, a smile in her voice.

Lou still lingered by the door, undoubtedly kept at a distance from her family friend by Mia's presence, but Mia hoped she would move farther into the store as Mia left so she didn't have to pass too close.

Mia made her way out with her gaze glued safely to the shop's hardwood floor. Was Lou going to start turning up in all her happy spots? Even though it was irrational, Mia felt hunted, chased down. A layer of sweat had formed on the back of her neck and she had to take a few more deep breaths before she could start walking—and scout the streets of Newtown for a much-needed second Pink Bean location.

---

Mia impatiently waited for the theatre to open so she could sink into one of the plush chairs, lose herself in the movie, and forget about reality for a few hours. She hadn't seen any suitable locations on King Street for the second Pink Bean which meant they may have to start looking in the side streets, which Mia didn't think would be a good business idea. Newtown was different than Darlinghurst and the branch here would need to attract more foot traffic than the other Pink Bean, which could rely on regulars from the neighborhood to keep the books comfortably in the black.

During her first two weeks there, Mia had been amazed at the amount of regulars the Pink Bean had. The Newtown branch would not be like that. The population was much more transient, made up of students and tourists rather than young families of which the parents needed their daily shot of caffeine to make it to the end of another tiring day.

The beginning of an idea was brewing in the deep

recesses of her subconscious, an idea she couldn't put her finger on quite yet. She would need to let it percolate for a while longer before it made itself known.

More people were starting to arrive and Mia checked her watch. The previous screening should just about be finished and soon there would be stream of people coming out. Mia found a spot near the wall from where she could keep an eye on everything. Most of the small crowd waiting with her were staring at their phone screens, missing out on the glorious pleasure of people watching.

A woman arrived whom Mia vaguely recognized but she couldn't pinpoint from where. The woman didn't give any signs of knowing her, so Mia tried shooting her a quick smile, but the woman's eyes remained just as glazed over. She glanced around furtively, scanning the queue. She was obviously meeting someone.

Then, from around the corner, appeared a face Mia did recognize. *Oh Christ.* Lou was going to the same movie as she was. She quickly looked away, then peered back from under her lashes. She was hidden by a group in front of her, so she could observe how Lou greeted the woman who had arrived earlier. Their hello was awkward. Not the greeting of people who'd known each other for a long time. A hesitant kiss on the cheek, not sure where to put the hands, stalling conversation and shy smiles.

This was a date.

Wait a minute. That woman. Now that she tilted her head and shot Lou a seductive smile… Had Mia seen her on Tinder the other day? She'd been feeling agitated because of the events with Lou that week, so she'd let Pat set up a profile for her on the dating app and then had promptly proceeded to swipe left on every single picture she saw. Truth be told, she had stalled at the woman who was now buying drinks for herself and Lou, had found something intriguing about her, but Mia didn't need a dating app to get a date. She'd go to the Newtown Hotel on a Tuesday night, order a beer, sit at the bar, and get her date the old-fashioned way—as opposed to quickly judging someone simply on how she looked—thank you very much.

So Lou was on Tinder as well—if she was right about this set-up. She was only guessing, and she was giving herself a lot of leeway in her guessing game, but it could be possible. This was the twenty-first century after all, and everything was possible.

It was her bad luck that the movie she'd chosen to see today was only playing at this theatre. It had obviously appealed to Lou and her date as well, making them end up in Mia's stomping ground. Her safe space, where she was the new Mia and nothing of the old one was let in.

Thank goodness the very nature of sitting in a movie theatre meant surrendering to the dark and to the lives depicted on the screen. Mia hoped the movie would be absorbing enough to allow her to forget about Lou's presence. If not, a Sunday afternoon visit to the Newtown Hotel was on the cards. And she wouldn't try to get a date with anyone there—not only because Sundays were not a favorite going out day amongst Newtown lesbians, but mostly because a date was the last thing on Mia's mind when she was in a mood like this, forced upon her by the actions of her past self.

The doors to the theatre opened and Mia rushed in, hoping that the seat she had been allocated would be far away from Lou's. She stepped into the familiar dark of the cinema, but only felt a fraction of the exhilaration that usually befell her every time she crossed the threshold. She briefly considered walking out, exchanging her ticket for another showing, and forgetting all about Lou. But she braced herself, told herself this was a dark room designed for forgetting about the other people who were sitting in there with you. The alternative was going home and moping, or walking around aimlessly. Moping wasn't going to get her anywhere.

She found her seat and forced herself not to look around. A few minutes later, she saw Lou and the woman walk past. Good. At least they were sitting in front of her and she didn't have to worry about Lou's eyes boring into the back of her head for the length of the movie. They sat down diagonally from Mia a few rows in front of her. Mia had no idea if Lou had clocked her. If she had, she didn't let on. Just as she had given zero signs of recognition at Annie's. As if Mia didn't exist and when Lou looked at her all she saw was a blank space.

Now that they were all seated, Mia couldn't help but watch the backs of their heads. Lou's long hair tied into a ponytail. The other woman's hair dirty blonde and short, her head bopping this way and that in an animated fashion. They were giggling about something. How strange to come to the cinema on the very first date—if that was really what this was. To sit next to each other in the dark and not be able to speak for two hours.

She saw Lou in profile and, out of nowhere, it hit her again how beautiful she had become. How Mia had reacted to meeting her before their past had been unveiled. Perhaps it hadn't been instant attraction, but if not that, then at least something very close to it. The woman sitting next to her must be over the moon. Mia wondered whether, if things hadn't been the way they were between her and Lou, she would be the one sitting next to her in this theatre right now. She had certainly been on a path to ask Lou out. She hadn't wanted to rush things because of her new job at the Pink Bean and her hopes had quickly been thwarted by Lou's cold demeanor toward her, but that first week, when Mia had been none the wiser, the thought had definitely occurred to her. Now, she sat watching Lou on a date with someone else. And was that woman truly so much better than Mia? At this stage of her life, when Mia had turned everything around, had grown out of the malice that she carried with her for those few years in high school, was she not just as worthy to go on a date with a woman she was attracted to?

Maybe she should fire up that Tinder app later on and give it a second chance. If women like Lou were to be found on there, Mia should give it another go.

## Chapter Eleven

At first sight, Meredith was lovely, but it was hard to focus on what she was saying with Mia Miller's eyes burning a hole into Lou's back. As Lou sat there, she was hyperaware of Mia's presence in the cinema. Even though she couldn't see her from where she sat—she had spotted her a few rows farther up when she and Meredith were searching for their seats—she could feel her. Lou was of half a mind to suggest skipping the movie and moving on to the dinner portion of this date, but when they had been texting earlier today, Meredith had been very enthusiastic about it and had emphasized that the movie would soon go out of circulation and this afternoon was the only chance they had of getting their minds blown by it on the big screen.

Lou had switched on her phone that morning with more urgency than usual. And she knew the reason for her eagerness: the possibility of something. As soon as her phone had booted up and she'd switched on the Tinder app, there it had been: a message from Meredith. Lou had immediately come clean and told her about knowing Robin, upon which Meredith had answered she knew very well who Lou was.

*Your recent, refreshing, and utterly beguiling presence in and around the Pink Bean has not gone unnoticed,* Meredith had messaged back.

Lou figured it must be the poet in her. She couldn't remember seeing Meredith at the Pink Bean, but perhaps she had been at the only other open mic night Lou had attended. Then, she had still been in restoration mood and hadn't taken much notice of anyone around her; instead she had listened to Phil and Jared as they tried to cheer her up.

Meredith talked fast and laughed raucously at the witticisms that kept spouting from her own mouth. She seemed to Lou a woman who was used to hanging with the high-testosterone boys at work, smart-talking her way out of everything. After only five minutes of initial, rather awkward conversation, it was clear that, on the surface at least, they were very different people. Which Lou considered a good thing. She needed someone with opposite character traits. Someone brash and bold and willing to coax her out of her shell. And if that someone had a poetic heart, all the better for it.

But, damn it, first she'd bumped into Mia at Annie's bookshop, and then again at the movie theatre. Would she never get a break from Mia Miller? Not even on a Sunday?

Annie had told her that Mia lived close by and had been coming to her bookshop for years, buying a book every single week—"Even when she looked as if she'd be much better off putting her money toward a good meal instead of more reading material," Annie had said. "Such a nice girl," Annie had continued, "who couldn't wait to get out of here as soon as you walked in. Have you been busy since you got back from Brisbane?"

Lou had shrugged off her mother's old friend's comments and had bought a book herself, even though she had a big to-be-read pile on her nightstand and was just in the middle of one. But for some insane reason she felt she couldn't leave the shop without buying something if that was what Mia had done. She had merely popped in to say hello to Annie. She hadn't been in this neighborhood for a while and she'd been curious as to how the shop was doing. Her reason for buying a book she was pretty sure she had spotted on her parents' bookshelves was utterly ludicrous. Now it burned a hole in her bag, along with Mia Miller's eyes in the back of her head.

But Lou was glad she was here with Meredith. That Mia could see she was a fully functioning adult who had no problem getting a date if she wanted to. Because ever since that conversation at Glow, that harrowing confrontation that had left her feeling a mixture of relief and inexplicable dread afterward, she had started thinking about Mia in a slightly different way.

Now that the shock of seeing her again had died down, along with the slew of bad memories Lou hadn't allowed herself to dredge up for the past decade, she could see Mia in another light. She was the kind of person most people reacted to in a positive manner because of the kindness she projected. Last night at Martha's, when they'd been scrolling through profile pictures on Tinder, Lou's gut reaction, before the one induced by trauma even had a chance to set in— before her brain realized it was a picture of Mia she was looking at—had been, if only for a fraction of a second, *what an attractive woman.*

More forceful sentiments had quickly taken over from that initial impression, but when she'd seen a woman with a charismatic smile and an easy manner—Mia again—talk to Annie in her shop earlier, she had remembered the thought from the night before. It had jolted her. And revolted her. Either you couldn't tell by looking at her that she was a bully, or Mia truly had transformed herself.

Then later, for someone like Lou who simply didn't enjoy

going to a movie on her own, seeing Mia wait to go in by herself had struck another chord with her. Mia had been far from the only person waiting in solitude, but there had been something about her as she stood there with her shoulder leaning against the wall, trying to conceal that she knew Lou was there as well. Something so vulnerable, Lou would never have associated it with Mia. And for a split second, the thought had popped into her brain: maybe Mia was a victim too.

A thought she'd quickly shaken off, not only because she had a date to impress, but also because it was a thought she wasn't willing to entertain. Because it didn't matter.

Once the movie had started Meredith had gone silent and she'd sat stock still, completely entranced by what was happening on the screen. But Lou couldn't focus all her attention on the shenanigans of the lovesick protagonist. Instead, she moved around in her seat and glanced behind her.

It was hard to make out Mia's face in the feeble light, yet Lou found it easily. She was staring straight at the screen—which was really all Lou wanted to find out with this maneuver. But then, just before Lou turned back, Mia must have felt Lou looking at her and their gazes connected across the darkened room. Lou quickly turned around. Meredith's attention had been drawn away from the screen and she sent Lou a quick smile, then refocused on the movie.

---

"I know her too," Meredith whispered in Lou's ear as they made their way out of the theatre. "Lesbian Tinder is like a small village."

"Who?" Lou didn't immediately know who Meredith was talking about.

"The woman you were looking at earlier and who just turned the corner." She gave a chuckle. "I'll be honest. I swiped right, but she obviously didn't feel the need to do so in response to my picture."

"I don't know her from Tinder. She works at the Pink Bean," Lou said.

"Really? She must be new then."

"She is." Lou confirmed, taken aback by the fact that she and her date were actually talking about Mia. Everywhere she went, no matter what she did: Mia. And of course Meredith had swiped right. And Lou had swiped right on Meredith and this was the world they lived in now. Swiping left or right could have a lasting effect on your future.

It was strange to go back to dating after being in a relationship for seven years. The way dating in itself had changed, Lou might as well have started dating Angie in another lifetime. They had met the *old-fashioned* way. At a party thrown by mutual friends. Not that Lou wanted to pass judgment on one way being better than the other, but things had changed so much. In a way, the internet and online dating was a blessing for her, because at parties she didn't always have the repartee and quick-wittedness to stun her conversation partners. She was the quiet, observing type. Definitely never the life of any party—in fact, after she'd met Angie and they had moved in together, Lou would have been fine with giving most parties a miss. At least the noisy, boisterous ones with too many people crammed into too small a space. Lou would take a small, civilized dinner party over that kind of set-up every day of the week.

"We're not our parents just yet," Angie used to say. "Put your glad rags on, babe. We're going dancing." And Lou did go dancing and enjoyed it most of the time, but not always, not like Angie who came alive under a spotlight and under the gaze of her friends.

They took an Uber to a restaurant not far from Meredith's apartment near the CBD. Lou had suggested the restaurant as a compromise: close to where Meredith lived, but serving excellent vegetarian food for her, according to the reviews.

"So I'm your first date, huh?" Meredith asked as they sat across from each other in the restaurant. "That doesn't bode well for me." She followed up with a chuckle.

"Why not?"

"What are the odds of you finding love again on the first date after your relationship ended?"

"I'd say those odds are not greater or smaller than on any other date. But maybe you know more about odds than I do because of your profession."

"Not when it comes to this, so I'll go with your view on things. And, by the way, do tell what kind of dirt Robin dished on me?"

This made Lou laugh. "Nothing too salacious. But I do know you write poetry and can often be found reading it at Pink Bean open mic nights."

"True enough. Did she review my poetry for you?"

Lou shook her head. "Nope. I guess I'll have to come to your next reading to find out what it's like for myself."

"You should." Meredith picked up her glass of wine and peered at Lou over the rim with her intense brown eyes.

She really was quite attractive. A completely different kind of woman than Angie, who had short-cropped hair and a half-dozen rings in her ear. That was the most astounding thing about Angie becoming such a slave to the corporation she worked for. She had always looked like the kind of person who would be out protesting the might of big business, not working for it.

Lou raised her glass as well. She clinked it gently against Meredith's and said, "I think I will."

The food arrived and, scoring many points in her favor, Meredith didn't ask Lou why she was a vegetarian. She just accepted it, and had ordered a meat-free dish as well. Lou had just picked up her knife and fork when Meredith's phone started ringing.

Meredith snapped to attention immediately. "I'm sorry. That's my work phone. I need to take this."

Lou had noticed that Meredith had two phones. Lou was the kind of person who would often, and gladly, leave her phone at home if she could. Going on a date with two devices in her bag was just unfathomable to her.

Meredith got up and went outside. Lou watched her gesticulate wildly through the window and wondered what could possibly be so important on a Sunday evening that it warranted such an agitated phone call from someone at work. She didn't have to wonder very long, because she knew if you were that kind of person, it was so easy to come up with a valid enough reason to interrupt dinner with a loved one—or in this case a prospective romantic interest. Angie had done it to her numerous times in the past few years and whereas Lou could understand that some things couldn't wait—although she couldn't possibly conjure up what those things could actually be, no matter how hard she tried, or how many times Angie explained it to her—she always felt for the person who had to take the call and had their life interrupted for no good reason.

What would happen if Meredith hadn't taken this call? Would the Australian economy go bust? Would the world stop turning? Would anyone truly think any less of her and if they did for that very reason, did it matter?

Lou shuffled uneasily in her seat as the memories of fights with Angie she had tried to forget made their way to the front of her mind once more.

"You're different," Angie used to say. "You're not made

for high-powered corporate environments, and I love that about you. I need to be with someone like you. Someone calm and quiet and balanced."

Angie hadn't noticed how out of balance her change of pace had thrown Lou. Of course she hadn't. She was too busy to notice. Because Lou definitely believed that idle hands were the devil's play thing, and that while work could have a lot of value in a person's life, it should never come at the cost of a relationship. It shouldn't continuously make your partner feel second best.

Meredith walked back into the restaurant with the kind of apologetic smile on her face Lou found hard to resist. She was already smiling back, when Meredith said, "I'm so very sorry, but I'm going to have to go."

"What?" Lou scoffed incredulously.

"That was the big boss. I would explain to you exactly what is going on right now, but I'm going to save you from that." Another smirk. Great. She was being condescending as well. "Sadly, I need to go to the office."

"It's Sunday evening."

"Don't I know it. But one of our analysts just discovered that—" She stopped herself. "Can I take a rain check on dinner?" She grabbed her purse and took out her wallet. "I'll pay for this, of course."

"I'll take care of it and no, you can't take a rain check." Lou was not interested in dating an even worse workaholic than Angie.

"Really? I thought things were going well." Meredith tried to grab the waiter's attention.

"Emphasis on *were*," Lou said with all the coldness in her voice she could muster.

"I'm really not blowing you off, if that's what you think. There is a genuine emergency at work. In fact, I really need to go now. I'm very sorry. I'll call you." Meredith stood shuffling around for a few more seconds, her face contorted with doubts and the realization that she had blown it.

"Don't bother," Lou said. She asked the waiter if she could take her meal home, paid, and left the restaurant feeling silly and sad.

———

Her parents were just stacking the dishes in the dishwasher when Lou walked into the kitchen.

"I wasn't expecting you home so early," her father said.

"Have you eaten? I have leftovers," her mother asked.

Lou held up the plastic bag with the take-out container. "The date was rudely interrupted."

"What happened?" her dad asked.

Lou scoffed. "She got called away by work. On a Sunday evening. Can you believe that?"

"I'm so sorry, honey," her mother said. "Did you like her?"

"I kind of did." Lou sank into a chair and lifted the lid of a pot that was standing in the middle of the table. She got a whiff of what was inside and her stomach started growling. She'd barely had the time to have a single bite of food before Meredith's phone had started ringing. "But I have no desire to see her again."

Her father sat at the table next to her. "Better luck next time," he said.

It was kind of funny to hear her dad say these words to her with such conviction in his tone. She knew he meant it, that all he wanted was for Lou to be the happiest she could possibly be, but it was just the way he said it. Like he was her best buddy instead of her father.

"Let's talk about something else," Lou said. "I stopped by Annie's shop this afternoon. It's not doing well."

"I know." Her mother sat as well. "I was talking about it with Beryl this afternoon. Her son overheard us and he said we should set up a crowdfunding campaign to save the shop."

Lou nodded. Her mother put a hand on her shoulder. "Are you sure you're all right, honey?" She'd been asking that question more than usual ever since Lou had told her parents that she had run into Mia Miller.

"I'm fine. I'd just like to do something for Annie, but I don't know what. She's had that shop for almost twenty years." She pursed her lips together. "Let me think about the crowdfunding idea for a bit." She delved into her bag and dug up the book she'd bought. "I couldn't help myself. Couldn't leave her shop without buying something."

Her dad picked up the book. "My copy was beginning to fall apart. We can do with a new one."

"Thanks, Dad." Lou was grateful that her father was not the kind of guy who would make her feel bad about buying a book they already owned. He would probably have bought it himself if he'd been in Annie's shop and just heard about her plight.

A silence fell and she caught a passing glance between her parents.

"What's going on?" she asked.

"Angie called again," her mother said on a sigh.

"Oh Christ. What did she say now?"

"The usual things. She's sorry. Could I talk to you on her behalf. She's going to change. On and on," her mother said.

"I'm sorry you had to listen to that." Lou rubbed her palms against her eyes. "What did you say to her?"

"I mostly listened. Then I told her you had made your decision."

"I made my decision six months ago. It's about time she starts accepting it."

"She's upset because she realizes she made a big mistake," her father chimed in.

"And I'm upset because I saw her change in front of my very eyes. She turned into someone else entirely. Someone I had no desire to be with anymore."

"I know, Lou. I know." Her father grinned awkwardly. "It's a difficult situation." Her father was the sensitive kind of person who had trouble holding back his own tears when Lou cried. After things had gone awry with Angie, there had been no doubt in Lou's mind about where to go: home. Her sanctuary. The place where she'd always been able to blot out what happened outside the four walls of the house. The house where her parents lived, the people who would always be her mother and father but to whom Lou could speak as though they were friends. A fact Angie was well aware of, and was now putting to her own use.

"I'll call her. Tell her to stop harassing you," Lou said.

Her mother nodded, then looked her in the eye. "You're absolutely, one hundred percent certain you don't want to give her another chance?" Her mother had always been fond of Angie. But Lou had yet to introduce her mother to a person she didn't instantly take to. She was the gregarious one of the Hamiltons. The woman with a dozen hobbies and a circle of friends and acquaintances so big, Lou could never remember all their names. Her mother was also the sort of woman who would always give everyone a second and then a third chance.

"I have been sure for a long time. It was over months before I left. We've talked about this." Lou couldn't keep a touch of irritation out of her voice.

"I know, darling. Just double-checking."

"Do you honestly believe she wants to change? If she's so desperate to make you believe she does, why isn't she here? It's not that long a flight from Brisbane. Why doesn't she take the time to come here and put her money where her mouth is?"

"Probably because she knows that it truly is too late. Because she knows you," Lou's father said. "But something inside her wants to keep trying."

"It's guilt. Pure and simple guilt. She screwed up and that's hard to live with. My guess is she doesn't really want to make any effort to get back together with me. She just wants me to absolve her. Take away her guilt. Tell her it wasn't all her fault."

"She wants forgiveness. That's only human," her mother said.

"Maybe one day I will forgive her. Who knows?" Lou took a deep breath. She spent a lot of time thinking about forgiveness, because she knew it was the only true path to happiness. To let all the things that weighed heavy on her soul go. But Angie's weight on her soul was still too crushing. And she'd need a few more dates with non-workaholics to lighten it.

## Chapter Twelve

"Can I ask you something?" Micky said. "Even though I might be speaking out of turn." She had invited Mia to her home instead of Glow to have another go at the advertising for the yoga studio.

"Of course you can." Here we go, Mia thought.

"It's just that Amber asked me to either not ask for your help with these ads, or if I did, to not have you over at Glow. She seems to have a grudge against you all of a sudden and Amber is not the kind of person who holds grudges. And for the life of me, I can't figure out why. I can come up with some theories, which I have done and confronted her with, but she's so secretive about all of it. Determined as well. I just can't wrap my head around it. And it makes for a bit of an unpleasant atmosphere."

Mia sighed. She had expected this question to arise from someone affiliated with the Pink Bean at some point. For an unknowing bystander it must come across as strange for Lou to be giving her the cold shoulder, and especially for Amber to join in. She wondered if Amber had told her girlfriend Martha. She seemed like the overly principled kind who wouldn't—which was good news for Mia. And she obviously hadn't confided in Micky. But how to explain this to her without Micky going off her as well?

"It's about Lou. We went to school together and we have a, er, rather unpleasant history."

"I figured as much. When were you in school together?"

"Fifteen years ago."

Micky quirked up her eyebrows. "First teenage love gone wrong?" she asked.

Mia shook her head. "If only."

"You don't have to give me the details, Mia," Micky said. "At least now I know something."

"I was horrible to Lou. Truly, truly horrible." Mia ignored Micky's words, because she wanted to give her more information. Saying it out loud might take away some of the power of the emotions that had been warring inside of her ever since that confrontation with Lou. The emotions that made her reconnect, on a nightly basis, with the bully she once was. It was hard to get a good night's sleep when she could still see young Louise Hamilton's face in front of her, contorted with tears and agony and frustration. All of which she had been the cause of.

"But it was fifteen years ago. What could you possibly have done to her for it to still have such an effect on her now? And moreover, for Amber to be dragged into it? I know Amber through and through and that's just not her style. I understand her allegiance would lie with Lou, because she has really taken to her, but this kind of silent animosity is the opposite of what Amber would do in any other situation."

A knot formed in the pit of Mia's stomach. Could she confide in Micky? If she told the story in her words, on her terms, would she understand?

"I bullied Lou," she said with a trembling voice. "All throughout our last year at Queen Mary. Almost every day, me and my gang would call her names because she didn't look like us, even though that was not the real reason, of course. We did it because we were scared and insecure teenagers and all I ever heard at home was what a shame it was that not all Aboriginals had been exterminated yet. Words uttered by my father who felt so uncomfortable in his own skin, he had to take it out on others. I'm not making excuses. Because for an entire year, every morning, I made the conscious decision to pick on a girl whose skin was darker than mine, just because my father did the same. I should have been wiser. But I ignored the bad feeling it gave me in my gut and continued, hoping for something to happen, although I never figured out what. It was cruel and childish and it ruined another person's life. And I am so ashamed of that person I was back then. But I'm not her anymore."

"I know you're not." Micky's voice had grown small. "You grew up in a house full of hate."

"Still, I was not stupid. I had a mind of my own that worked perfectly well. Even though I failed my last year and had to do it again, which didn't help with my anger issues."

"Have you told this to Lou? Or at least to Amber?"

"No, of course not. I don't want to make excuses for my behavior." Mia's voice broke. "You should have seen Lou when she sat me down and confronted me. Should have heard the things she said when she talked about the effect my bullying had on her." A tear made its way down Mia's cheek. She wiped it away.

"I can understand it might have been a shock to see you, and that you and Lou will never be best friends, but it happened fifteen years ago. How old were you? Seventeen? Chris is approaching that age and although he's very mature for a sixteen-year-old, a lot of the time, he's still just a child. And the mind of a child is so influenceable. I don't mean to absolve you of all the blame. What you did was wrong. I just don't think you should still be punished for it now. Kids get bullied. Life is hard. So many things that shouldn't happen, do happen, leave scars, hurt people. That's the very essence of life, just like making mistakes is, and learning from them."

"I'm not sure I deserve your kindness." Micky's words stunned Mia.

"It's not kindness, Mia. It's common sense. A mother's common sense." She expelled a sigh. "Do I have your permission to talk to Amber about this? You are helping us. You are helping our business, yet she won't have a simple conversation with you. That's not right." She straightened her back. "If people can't be forgiven for the mistakes they made in the past, if we keep on treating them like the people who made that mistake years later, and fail to give them a second chance, how can we ever expect them to truly change?" Micky shook her head. "Look at you, Mia. You may not feel like one right now, but you're a beautiful person. You are kind and helpful and full of good will. I may not have known you for that long, but I know *that* much."

"Thank you," Mia uttered.

"Have you talked about these things with anyone after they happened?" A concerned tone took over Micky's voice.

Mia shook her head in quick bursts. "I couldn't talk about it. I was too ashamed."

"That's the sort of shame that will eat you alive if you don't address it." She tilted her head. "So, what do you say? Can I tell Amber about this conversation?"

This impromptu talk with Micky was making Mia realize she'd been holding on to a lot of tension ever since that evening at Glow. She tensed up every time Lou or Amber turned up at the Pink Bean. She had her guard up when she simply walked from the bus stop to the coffee shop, fearing she might run into them and get an earful. Emotions Lou must have been so familiar with back when they were in school together.

Mia didn't feel comfortable with Micky doing her bidding for her, but Amber wouldn't talk to her—at least she didn't give the impression that she would stoop so low anytime soon—and if Mia was going to function in this community, and in life in general, perhaps something did need to be done. And Micky was a great ally to have.

"Okay. Only Amber, though. Don't tell Lou about this. If we do ever talk again, I want to be the one to open up to her. I owe her that much."

"I won't tell Lou. Chances are she wouldn't want to hear it, anyway. But Amber is my best friend. She needs to know this. Truth be told, I'm surprised she hasn't asked you about this."

"Thank you." Mia was feeling a little overwhelmed. "I should go now. Leave you to it."

"Leave me to what? My children are with their father and Robin's out with Meredith." She pursed her lips together. "Meredith went on a date with Lou and it didn't end very well. From what I gathered she's trying to recruit Robin to put a good word in with Lou. Give her a second chance." Micky rose. "How about more wine?"

Mia's brain worked furiously as she nodded. It was only Tuesday. Surely Lou hadn't been on any other dates since Sunday. So she had guessed right. The only thing she couldn't figure out was how Meredith had screwed up the date. They'd looked quite chummy in the cinema.

"I would love more wine." Mia wasn't looking forward to the bus ride back to Newtown. Especially as she had to take the same bus in the other direction at six o'clock tomorrow morning. She'd best go easy on the wine.

"You're welcome to stay in Liv's room," Micky said, as

though reading her mind. "I know what those early mornings are like."

---

"Oh, please, Mia," Jo said. "I commuted from Newtown to Darlinghurst every single weekday morning for two years."

"Yes, well, you had a car to take you around, which I don't."

"A car that saved me a lot of dough because of not having to pay for the ridiculously expensive and ineffective Sydney public transport system." Jo was in a feisty mood this morning. "What did you do for knickers, anyway? Did you wash them out in the sink?"

Mia flashed Jo a wide smile. "Even better. I'm not wearing any."

"I'm pretty sure you're breaking some hygiene law just by standing here. I should report you to Kristin."

"Like it has never happened to you." Mia scrutinized Jo's face. "What with your *lover* having her fancy digs so nearby."

"I have a drawer now. Well, much more than a drawer. A corner of the dressing room. I don't have nearly enough clothes to fill up my part."

"How long have you two been together now?"

"About eight months," Jo said.

"I'm surprised you haven't moved in yet."

"Frankly, I'm a little surprised myself. Caitlin has asked me, and I practically live there. I stay with her about ninety percent of the time, but it's hard to leave Camperdown. I've lived there ever since I moved to Sydney and as rickety as my flat is, it's a good spot to have while I'm doing my PhD." She sighed. "Or maybe I'm just not ready to move in with Caitlin. I've never been one to make an impulsive decision."

"Do you know that bookshop on King Street. Annie's?" Mia asked.

Jo nodded. "Of course. It's a Newtown institution. I actually bought my now-signed copies of Caitlin's books there years ago."

"I was there this weekend and Annie was telling me how she has had yet another offer from Pages. One she is inclined to take. Not whole-heartedly, but because she's not sure there's a lot of use in fighting any longer."

"Oh come on. Not Annie's. Will there be no independent bookshops left in this city?"

The front door opened and Micky, Amber, and Lou walked in. Mia's muscles tensed immediately. She wondered if Micky had had a chance to talk to Amber yet.

"How are you feeling this morning, Mia?" Micky asked. "Personally, I'm not feeling all too well." She brought her hands to her head. "Your colleague drank me under the table last night," she said to Jo.

"I know all about it." Jo shot Mia a quick wink. "Too much information included."

"I feel fine," Mia said from behind the coffee machine, where she had taken the habit of hiding as best she could as soon as Amber and Lou walked in.

"At least that makes one of us," Micky said and paid for the drinks. "We'll be at our usual table."

After Jo had brought the three of them their beverages—a pattern they had wordlessly fallen into because Jo had excellent intuition when it came to detecting tension, and Mia had made her understand, without trying to give anything away, that she was not comfortable serving Amber and Lou—she brought the subject of conversation back to Annie's bookshop.

"I'm just as guilty as the next person," Josephine said. "I haven't been in there for a good number of months. Not that

I ever have a lot of spare cash to spend on books I don't need for work."

"I don't think we should be naive about it. People buy their books, be it digital or print, mostly on Amazon these days. And if not on Amazon, then at a big chain like Pages. That's the reality of an industry in flux. Annie's shop is based on a business model that can't be saved, not the way it has been operating for the past eighteen years. But she said that Pages want to turn it into an independent-looking branch of their shop, which means that they do see value in the image of the indie shop." Mia sighed. "I feel there's an idea in there somewhere, but it hasn't fully formed in my head yet." She glanced at Josephine. "You're a smart cookie. If we put our heads together, maybe we can come up with something."

"I'm doing a PhD in Gender Studies. I don't have that much of a mind for business."

"Er, excuse me."

Mia and Jo looked up. Mia had recognized the voice, of course, but she could hardly believe Lou was standing in front of the counter. She left the ordering up to Amber and Micky whenever she could.

"Are you talking about Annie's bookshop in Newtown? I'm sorry, I couldn't help but overhear."

"We are," Jo confirmed. "We are mortified that it might disappear."

"So am I. I've known Annie all my life. She's a friend of my mother's. We were talking about the bookshop at home over the weekend and someone suggested that Annie set up a crowd-funding campaign."

"Crowd-funding?" Jo said.

Mia was still too flabbergasted at being involved in a conversation with Lou to respond quickly.

"I honestly don't know the first thing about it, although Jimmy suggested we do a Kickstarter campaign to collect funds to record a proper album," Jo said. "What do you and your MBA think, Mia?"

"I think crowd-funding would work very well in your case, Jo, but for saving a bookshop, I'm not sure. It would be throwing money at something that could never become viable again on its own merits. You'd have to do campaign after campaign and that's no model to base a business on."

"Hm, maybe you're right," Lou said.

"Here's an idea," Jo offered. "All three of us want to do something. We should get Kristin involved because she has a nose for business. Have a meeting and brainstorm ideas."

"The Save Annie's Bookshop Committee," Mia said.

"She will surely want to help. Sheryl and I used to go there together sometimes. Let's put some lesbian muscle behind this," Jo said with rising excitement in her voice. "Are you in?" she asked Lou.

Lou gave an adamant yes.

"So am I," Mia said. "I'll talk to Kristin today." That inkling of an idea she knew she was on the cusp of having had inched its way forward in her brain a little more. Even though, at that very moment, she couldn't pay as much attention to it as she wanted, because she had to process the fact that she and Lou would be sitting at a table and discussing this together.

## Chapter Thirteen

Lou had just taught her last class of the day, which Kristin, Sheryl, Caitlin, Jo, and Micky had all attended.

"Since the Pink Bean is not open late yet, we'd best go back to mine," Caitlin said. "I have a fridge full of wine and a lovely balcony overlooking the city to drink it on. What do you say, girls?" Caitlin said.

Lou was tired and had planned an early night, but she'd heard so many tales of Caitlin's fancy penthouse that her curiosity won out over her fatigue. Besides, she really liked Caitlin. She had a big personality and a mouth to match it. And she obviously made Jo very happy.

"Sure, but just the one," Kristin said. "It's a school night, after all."

"And your better half has the early shift tomorrow," Jo said to Caitlin.

"My better half is also twenty years younger than me, so she can take it," Caitlin quipped. "How about you, Lou? Are you coming?"

"I would love to."

Wet-haired from their showers, they all headed to Caitlin's place. Micky fell into step next to Lou.

"I'll text Robin that we'll all be at Caitlin's so she can come over if she has any energy left after CrossFit." She looked at Lou. "And I'll tell her *not* to bring Meredith."

Micky had asked Lou all about her date with Meredith, and Lou had told her exactly how it had gone. After which Micky had told Lou she knew Meredith and her wouldn't be a good fit. She should have spoken up when they were all huddled over Lou's phone, getting overly excited by Tinder and its prospects, but she'd let herself get caught in the heat of the moment.

"Much appreciated," Lou said, able to have a chuckle about it now.

"Have you got anymore internet dates lined up?" Micky asked.

"God no. After the last one… I've learned that looks are the most deceiving thing, especially on the internet."

"I hear you," Micky said. "And there will be no more dates with any of Robin's colleagues or any banker for that matter."

"Don't you ever think Robin works too much?" Lou didn't know where she got the audacity to ask, but she was very keen to learn the answer.

"Not really," Micky said. "I was married to a person for whom the word 'workaholic' was an understatement. Compared to my ex-husband, Robin keeps very decent hours. It's all a matter of perspective really. Like so many things in life."

They arrived and the elevator was large enough to bring the six of them to the top floor comfortably. When she arrived at Caitlin's penthouse, Lou could barely believe her eyes. It looked like one of those homes you only ever saw in interior design magazines.

Wine was poured and Caitlin put a couple of frozen pizzas in the oven so they could share a nibble and then they all sat staring out over the city as darkness truly fell.

Sheryl was the only one who didn't drink, so Lou put two and two together quickly. She glanced at Kristin and wondered if Mia had managed to speak to her yet about a plan to save Annie's Bookshop.

Lou hadn't expected to walk up to her and Jo earlier that day, but she had, and she could only conclude that her feelings for Annie getting a fair deal were more important to her than her feelings toward Mia.

"Business at Glow seems good," Caitlin said to Micky, snapping Lou out of her reverie.

"We truly can't complain. Although that full class tonight was due to a lot of free trial members that have signed up very recently thanks to the wonders of very localized Google and Facebook advertising. Mia has been a real star for helping us with those."

"Mia is amazing," Kristin said. "Very smart, but not in the usual overbearing I've-been-to-business-school way, you know?"

"And she's much nicer to me than you ever were," Jo said to Micky, throwing in a giggle.

"Impossible. I always treated you like a queen," Micky replied.

Jo smirked, then said, "All jokes aside, I really like her. Are you keeping her, boss?" she asked Kristin.

Lou sat there wondering whether Micky had set this whole thing up so various people could vouch for Mia's character in her presence. She was pretty sure Mia was all the great things these women thought of her now, but she hadn't always been.

"I'm making her," Sheryl said. "She's too easy on the eye to let go."

Kristin slapped her partner on the thigh.

"I'm so disappointed in you, Sheryl," Jo said. "I might need to get a new thesis advisor. All the things I've always believed about you have come crumbling down just with that one shallow comment."

"Come on, Jo." Sheryl pointed at Kristin. "Look at my partner. Surely you must have known all along that I appreciate great beauty."

"There's no use in trying to flatter your way out of it," Kristin said.

"Well, you can all sit here and be holier than thou about it, but I won't for a split second believe nobody else here thinks she's a real hottie," Sheryl said.

"*A real hottie,*" Caitlin chimed in. "That's not the sort of language we use, Sheryl. What has become of you?" She stared at Kristin. "Is it the change? Has the time come?"

They all snickered and Lou was glad they'd stopped extolling the virtues of Mia's character. As long as they mainly talked about her looks, Lou wasn't inclined to see Mia in a different light.

"Her trial period is up at the end of the week and I will not be letting her go," Kristin said, ignoring Caitlin's remark. "I'll need to hire a new barista for the morning shift pretty soon." She glanced at Micky. "Unless you want to come back?"

Micky pursed her lips together. "Sorry, Kristin. I'm in the yoga business now. We all know Glow would fall apart without me." Micky glanced at Lou. Was she expecting her to back her up? Or was it an invitation to join in the banter between these old friends, amongst whom Lou still felt like a bit of an outsider?

"I can attest to that," Lou said and quickly sipped from her wine. "Amber and I would be in ruins if it weren't for Micky."

"Thank you." Micky tilted her head toward Lou.

Lou couldn't help but smile. Outsider status or not, it felt good to slowly become part of a group of friends here in Sydney. Mixing business with pleasure was part and parcel of being a yoga teacher, because regulars she got along with would often become acquaintances or more. That was the nature of the practice. Despite the matter of Mia, she was actually glad that Glow and the Pink Bean were two businesses so intertwined, they might as well have been dreamed up by the same person.

"Mia will do the morning shift for a while longer, but not too much longer," Kristin mused. "No offense to either of you, but I do feel her talents are wasted behind the coffee machine. In fact, she's pitching me an idea tomorrow."

Lou could guess what that idea was. She was also secretly relieved that the meeting between her, Jo, Kristin, and Mia hadn't been set up yet. It was all well and good to walk up to Mia and Jo spurred on by worry in a brief moment of temporary insanity, but Lou wasn't sure what actually sitting at a table with Mia would do to her. Although she figured she would need the practice. If she wanted to make her way from the outskirts of this group of friends to being warmly embraced by them, she would need to learn to at least be around Mia without flinching or giving away that there was no love lost between them.

Kristin was definitely hiring her. She would be at the Pink Bean regularly. It was simply the way things were. And the very last thing Lou wanted to do was cause a rift in this group. The ones who liked Mia—which turned out to be most of them—against the ones who didn't—she and Amber who were unwilling to openly state the reason for their dislike.

"None taken. I mean, I grew out of my job behind that coffee machine in no time," Micky said. "Although, strangely,

I do miss it sometimes. Not the getting up early, of course, but just being in the Pink Bean, hanging out with my buddy Josephine."

"Meeting hot ladies who order wet cappuccinos," Jo said.

"Just the one was fine with me," Micky said. "But really, working at the Pink Bean has changed my life."

"Opening the place has changed ours," Kristin said.

"We wouldn't know most of you if we hadn't," Sheryl said. "Although my hackles did go up once Kristin started talking about expansion and a liquor license and a new store."

"But that's why we have Mia," Kristin said.

"She can get quite obsessive about new projects, to the point that she neglects her wifely duties." Sheryl grinned at Lou.

Lou felt a mild blush creep up her cheeks. The Pink Bean might be a magical place for all of them, but it was decidedly not for Lou.

"Oh, stop it, you." Kristin patted Sheryl on the knee.

The banter continued, and Lou enjoyed being part of it, but she couldn't help but think it would all be so much easier if it wasn't for Mia Miller.

---

After the brief chat with Mia and the previous night's jolliness between the Pink Bean owners and a few of its patrons, Lou didn't feel so uneasy about going into the coffee shop. Mia never served her, anyway, and Lou was usually with Amber, who seemed to be warming up to Mia a little of late.

Lou hadn't spoken to her boss about Mia again, figuring she had already been enough of a nuisance to Amber. Apparently Mia was really helping Amber out. Some of the people in her classes were only there because of the ads Mia had set up. That was probably why Amber threw Mia a smile now and again and, earlier when they'd just arrived, had struck up a short conversation with Mia.

"I have to go," Amber said to Lou. "I'm meeting with a new ecological towel laundry service who want to flaunt their wares at me. Are you going to be all right on your own? You can always join me, if you like that sort of thing."

"I dislike sales pitches from the bottom of my heart," Lou said. She cast a glance at Mia who was sitting at a table working on her laptop. "Besides, I can always leave."

"That you can." Amber got up, said her goodbyes, and left.

Truth be told, Lou was glad for some time alone at a table in the Pink Bean. It gave her a chance to get used to being in the same space as Mia, without having to talk to her.

She delved in her bag for her book, but instead of opening it, the book drew her mind to Annie and her shop again. This, in turn, made her glance over at Mia, who was deeply focused on whatever she was doing on her laptop. Maybe she was working on a plan to save Annie's shop at that very moment. Most likely she was working on the idea she was slated to pitch to Kristin.

"Hey." A voice came from the other side of Lou's table. A voice she vaguely recognized.

Lou turned away from Mia and stared into Meredith's face.

"Can we talk for a minute?" Meredith asked. "Can I get you a coffee? I owe you for dinner."

"You don't owe me a thing."

Meredith pulled back a chair and sat down unbidden. "You won't reply to my messages, not even the ones I've sent through Robin."

"That should make things loud and clear." Instinctively,

Lou leaned away from the table they were now both sitting at.

"I'm really sorry about having to rush off like that last Sunday." She paused while her glance skittered away, then landed back on Lou. "I really, really like you, Lou."

"How did you even know I was here?" Lou didn't like the urgency in Meredith's tone.

"Your schedule is online. I figured you'd be here between classes. This is where everyone hangs out, isn't it?" She tried a smile. If she was going for disarming, it wasn't working.

Lou felt ambushed. She didn't want to talk to Meredith. She hadn't given her much more thought. It was a done deal for her.

"Look, will you go out with me again? We can just go for coffee. Just... let me prove to you that I'm not that person. We had chemistry. You can't deny that."

"I would like you to leave," Lou raised her voice only a fraction.

"Everything okay here?" Out of nowhere, Mia had appeared next to their table. She fixed her gaze on Lou. "Are you being harassed?"

"Harassed?" Meredith said. "We're just talking."

"Seems to me Lou doesn't feel much like talking."

"And who are *you*?" Meredith hissed, then narrowed her eyes. Maybe she recognized Mia from her Tinder picture and from seeing her at the cinema. "Are you two a thing now?" she asked. "Is that what all the misplaced chivalry is about?"

"I can handle myself, thank you," Lou spoke up. Oh, the irony of having Mia come to her rescue. "I would like you both to leave me alone."

"Ah, so not a thing. Are we both vying for your hand?" Meredith said.

"Neither one of you is vying for anything. I'm not interested, Meredith. I thought I had made that clear. And you." Lou looked at Mia, who had taken a step back. "Just… don't."

"Fine." Meredith rose, the feet of her chair scraping loudly against the floor. "Your loss," she mumbled and made her way out of the Pink Bean.

They both watched her skulk off. Then Mia said, "I'm sorry. I was out of line."

Lou sighed. "Oh, it's fine. It's just, well, you know."

"A little bit ironic given our history," Mia said.

Was she really going to go there?

"Quite." Lou didn't know what to say.

"Now that we're, uh, talking…" Mia shuffled her weight around. "I know I haven't gotten back to you about Annie's. I'm working on something, but I'd like to talk to Kristin about it in private first. Then we can discuss it further with you and Jo. I hope that's all right."

"Yeah, sure. I haven't been able to come up with any brilliant plans myself so… all our hopes rest on you." Lou actually felt compelled to smile at Mia.

Mia smiled back. "No pressure then."

"None."

"Micky tells me you're responsible for all those new people turning up in my classes. I, er, really appreciate your help. So does Amber."

"It's just a few ads." Mia waved her comment away. "It's really nothing."

"I just wanted you to know that your efforts are appreciated."

"That's nice to hear." Another smile. "I'll leave you to it now." Mia started walking off.

"Mia…" Lou suddenly thought it wholly unfair that she was the reason Mia was barely allowed into Glow.

"Yes?" Mia turned around and slid her hands into her jeans pockets.

"If you want to take some classes at Glow, please feel free to come."

Mia sent her a crooked grin. "That's okay. I'm not that much of a yoga person, anyway. But thanks for offering." Mia slunk off, looking like she had shrunk a few centimetres since she had stood towering over the table, trying to scare off Meredith.

Lou watched her and wondered if this was perhaps equally hard on Mia. To come face-to-face with a part of her past that must be difficult to reconcile with the person she had become. Because if there was one thing shining through as time progressed, it was that Mia Miller was a good person now. Either that, or she had half the population of Darlinghurst fooled—Lou included.

## Chapter Fourteen

"My idea is perhaps not in line with your vision for the second Pink Bean coffee shop, but I wanted to bring it up anyway," Mia started her pitch to Kristin. The idea had finally crystalized in her mind on a bus ride between the Pink Bean and her home.

"I'm all ears," Kristin said.

"There is this women's book shop in Newtown, Annie's."

"I know Annie's. I went there quite often when Sheryl and I lived near the university. Lovely woman, even though I haven't been there in a while," Kristin said.

This sounded like a promising first reaction to Mia. "The thing is, Annie's Bookshop is not doing very well and is about to close or be sold to Pages. I've been in plenty of bookshops that have a nook set aside where customers can buy a cup of coffee while they peruse the book they've just bought, or might buy if they got to hold it in their hands for a while. Even the big branch of Pages in the CBD has one." Mia paused for a beat. "The more I think about it, the more I'm convinced that the Pink Bean and Annie's Bookshop could be a match made in heaven. An LGBT-friendly coffee shop plus a women's bookshop. A university with a thriving Gender Studies department a stone's throw away. If there's one thing students don't economize on—nor anyone else for that matter—it's a good cup of coffee. The Pink Bean could have its perfect Newtown venue and Annie's could survive."

Mia watched Kristin's face for signs of excitement or dismissal. But Kristin was a master at not showing her feelings and didn't give much away of what she thought about Mia's somewhat crazy idea.

"So how do you see this working practically? Would the two businesses be co-existing in the same location?"

"That's one option. We could lease part of the space from Annie and draw customers to her bookshop. Or we could buy her out and have her lease the space from us. I have done the numbers for both scenarios. But, perhaps, some sort of trial run first would be best."

"In theory, it's not a bad idea," Kristin said, not dismissing the idea outright, "but I'll need some time to mull it over, talk to Sheryl, visit the shop." Kristin wasn't one to bubble over with enthusiasm at the most festive of times, so Mia considered this a win.

"Of course."

"Can you find out how time sensitive this is?" she asked. "Is Annie on the verge of accepting an offer or just considering it?"

"I'll go by later today and find out for you."

"Thanks." Kristin painted a big smile on her face. "On another note, I'm very happy to inform you that when your trial period ends later this week, I would like to make you an official employee. If you're interested in becoming a permanent member of the Pink Bean team, that is."

Kristin had invited Mia to dinner to celebrate her trial period being over. Mia had been up to the flat before, but she'd never been afforded the opportunity to take such a long, satisfying glimpse into her employers' private lives.

"Champagne or no champagne?" Sheryl asked.

"Champagne, of course. This is a celebration," Kristin said. "I'll take care of it."

"Sparkling water for me." Sheryl grinned at Mia, her eyes lingering a little longer than Mia thought perhaps necessary. "I prefer to be upfront about this to erase the speculation from people's minds: yes, I'm a recovering alcoholic. No, I don't mind you drinking in my company."

Mia nodded. "Got it."

Kristin returned with the champagne, popped the cork, and poured Mia a glass.

"To Mia Miller," she said.

"Thank you very much." After taking a quick, polite sip, Mia said, "I must say this is the first time an employer has cracked open the champagne for an occasion like this."

"We're lucky to have you," Kristin said.

"I'm just glad she likes you," Sheryl said. "Kristin is just as much a recovering workaholic as I am a plain old alcoholic. She needs someone like you working at the Pink Bean."

Mia noticed Kristin shooting Sheryl a look she couldn't quite decipher.

"And I hear you have big plans," Sheryl said.

"Nothing bigger than is expected of me."

They spoke about the prospect of the Pink Bean merging with Annie's Bookshop for a while and forged a plan for Sheryl and Kristin to stop by over the weekend, without Annie being informed of their potential interest. Simply to look at the place with a different mindset, to walk in and imagine if it was possible.

"I take it you're enjoying working at the Pink Bean?" Sheryl, the more overtly inquisitive of the couple, asked. She had a very different way of asking questions than Kristin. More direct and, somehow, more probing. More demanding of a direct answer.

"I love it." Mia would say that, of course, but she genuinely had fallen for the Pink Bean. "It has a great vibe, amazing owners, and a wonderful bunch of customers. And I get along with Jo really well. I won't claim I jump out of bed in spritely fashion when my alarm goes off at five, because I'm so not a morning person, but once my day gets going, and I'm surrounded by the delicious smells of coffee, I feel very fortunate."

"This is a genuine love fest we have on our hands here tonight then." Sheryl waggled her eyebrows and, again, kept her gaze locked on Mia's for a second longer than politeness dictated. Maybe she was just that kind of person, or maybe Mia had been invited here tonight for other reasons than just a celebration. One glance at Kristin and she knew that was not the case. These two were so different—Kristin with her impeccable attire and measured movements and Sheryl in her eternal vests and her easy way—but yet so suited to each other.

"When it's a good fit, it's a good fit," Kristin said drily.

Mia remembered the day of her interview vividly. Kristin had been somewhat intimidating, yet Mia had seen more in her than the business-savvy, always-on-top-of-everything boss of the Pink Bean. Sheryl didn't ask any questions then, but just sat there observing and, Mia had concluded later, giving off a distinct lesbian vibe. Perhaps she had intimidated some other candidates, but not Mia.

Neither of them had come across as if they would hire Mia solely because of her easy smile and outgoing personality. Luckily, Mia had the right qualifications for the job along with a burning desire to work for a small outfit like the Pink Bean.

She didn't mind that she would earn less than at the previous company she had worked for, nor that there wasn't any sure path to promotion. She didn't care about any of that, as long as she was granted enough independence to work on her ideas to make the Pink Bean an even better place than it already was. Kristin and Sheryl might only have been hiring someone because Kristin needed help with her expansion plans, but Mia was someone with her own ideas and dreams and somehow, after she had walked into the coffee shop and shaken off most of her nerves, she had felt there was something special about the place.

"You should have heard everyone rave about you the other night after yoga," Sheryl said. "Throw it all together and one would easily believe you're the second coming of the Christ. Right here in Darlinghurst." She chuckled.

Mia's ears perked up at the sound of the word *yoga*. Did that mean Amber had been there? Amber, who knew about her past.

"Really? Please go on stroking my ego. I've been having such a great night of it already."

"Micky was saying how much you helped them with Glow's ads."

Ah. Micky. "It was only a couple hours of my time. And a good chance to schmooze with an ex-employee and loyal customer."

"I haven't seen you at any of the classes," Sheryl said. "Yoga has been a great help with my sobriety and Amber can talk almost anyone into at least giving it a go. I'm surprised she hasn't swayed you yet."

Did they know something? Were they trying to suss her

out, getting her to say something about the animosity between her and Lou, which must be palpable to two such observant people, especially to Kristin who watched the goings-on at the Pink Bean like a hawk? But the contract had been signed. They were drinking champagne to celebrate Mia's official appointment as Pink Bean manager. This was hardly the time to trap her into divulging information that could possibly get her fired.

"I—er." Mia hesitated, unsure what to say to her employers. Lou had promised that neither she nor Amber would tell anyone. "I've been a bit busy," she said.

"If you find the time to work on their ads, surely you have time to take one of their classes," Sheryl said, her eyes piercing, her tone probing.

"I guess. I'll get myself an acceptable yoga kit over the weekend and perhaps go next week." It was a lie, which made Mia feel uneasy.

"There's a class most of us take together on Saturday afternoon," Sheryl said. "Lou teaches it. Why don't you join us for that one? You can see it as a kind of Pink Bean team building exercise. Jo will be there, along with me and Kristin."

"Babe, leave it." Kristin put a hand on Sheryl's shoulder. "I'm sure Mia has much better things to do with her weekend than doing yoga with us." She fixed her gaze on Mia. "Please don't feel as if you need to do this." She cast Sheryl a stern glance. "I'm going to check on dinner."

Once Kristin had left the living room, Sheryl leaned in toward Mia and said, "We know something is going on between you and Lou. Something must have happened, but we can't quite put our finger on it. I promised Kristin I wouldn't push, that you would tell us if and when you felt the need, but I have less impulse control than my wife, so I'm asking you, woman to woman: what happened?"

A blush crept up Mia's cheeks. Sheryl's intense gaze was not one to easily avoid. She would have to give her something else than the lame excuse that yoga was not for her—even though, under any other circumstance, that would be perfectly acceptable.

"Lou and I knew each other in school." An awkward pause. "We weren't the best of friends."

"A feud at university?" Sheryl asked.

Mia shook her head. "High school. It was all my fault, but I'd rather not go into the specifics." She thought about what Lou had said a few days earlier, about Mia being welcome to take a class at Glow. Coming clean to Micky as they were drinking wine was one thing, but fessing up to Sheryl, with her demanding stare and the millions of questions she would have at the ready afterward—Mia was sure of this—was another thing entirely. This was not an intimate moment between her and a budding friend she had just done a favor. Sheryl was her boss. "I hope Lou and I can figure it out over time."

They had exchanged a few words since that painful night at Glow when Lou had confronted her. They would never be friends, but perhaps Lou, with her gentle character and her Zen attitude could find it in her heart to forgive Mia some day.

"So you're not ex-lovers gone awry?" Sheryl leaned back in her chair.

Mia managed a dry chuckle. "Nothing like that at all."

"And you won't be going at each other's throats in the middle of the Pink Bean any time soon?"

"Most certainly not." Mia hoped she had reassured Sheryl.

"Then you are exempt from yoga tomorrow afternoon." She shot Mia a smile.

"Maybe some other time." Mia smiled back.

"Dinner's ready," Kristin said from the kitchen.

"Let me be the one to tell Kristin I interrogated you further," Sheryl said as they headed toward the dining table. "She'll be able to handle it better if it comes from me."

## Chapter Fifteen

Lou had agreed to babysit the twins while Phil and Jared went to the opera. She had suggested it herself when the sitter they had booked weeks in advance had cancelled a few days ago. She wasn't planning on going on anymore Tinder dates any time soon, anyway.

While Jared prepared the twins for bed, she confided in Phil about the disastrous end to what had been a promising date with Meredith, how she had turned up at the Pink Bean out of the blue, and how Mia had come to her defense.

"She sure has a nerve," Phil said, while pouring them both a glass of wine as they stood around the kitchen island.

"Mia or Meredith?" Lou asked with a smile.

"Meredith has already been forgotten about." Phil knew all about Lou's unwillingness to ever again date someone who would even consider taking a work call during a Sunday night dinner.

"I didn't really take offense," Lou said. "There was something… strangely sweet about it."

"The wolf has purchased better sheep's clothing," Phil said.

"You should hear the others gush about her. I can't go anywhere these days without someone saying how utterly marvelous Mia Miller is. Like the universe decided to conspire against the harsh feelings I still harbor toward her."

"They can say all they want; they don't know what she's really like."

"But what is she really like, though?"

"What do you mean?" Phil gave her a puzzled look. He had blindly put all his allegiance behind Lou as soon as she'd told him about Mia's past antics.

"I'm beginning to think that she's not the same person anymore. These days, it seems she spends her days helping people, even trying to rescue Annie's Bookshop. She respects the boundaries I set completely, and then some. If anything, it's me who is making her feel excluded. It makes me wonder whether people can change. A notion I wasn't even willing to consider after seeing her again, but as time goes by, and I see more of her and what she's like today, I ask myself whether I'm the one being too hard on her now."

"Seriously?" Phil downed the wine he had just poured. "You're willing to forgive and forget?"

Lou shook her head. "No, of course not, but I'm not sure I'm willing to hate for much longer. Hate is just such a… corrosive emotion."

"You've been a yoga teacher for too long."

"Why are you giving me such a hard time about this?" Lou asked because this wasn't Phil's style. He was usually such an easy-going guy, willing to give everyone the benefit of the doubt.

"I'm doing no such thing, but I know you, Lou. I met you not long after you escaped Mia Miller's evil clutches, and you have come such a long way since then. You put yourself together again, but it took many long and hard years to do so. I wouldn't want to see that jeopardized in any way."

"But that's just the point. I've changed. I'm not that girl I once was. Maybe she has changed as well."

"She'd better have." Phil shook his head. "But the two are so completely different."

"I'm not so sure. We both had to change to survive."

"No, Lou, she changed you first by diminishing you and lowering your self-esteem and turning you into a nervous mess."

"I was already a nervous mess."

"That's of no importance." Phil cocked his head. "I feel like you have changed since the last time we spoke. Who is this person standing in the kitchen with me? Did Mia get to you in any way?"

"Don't be silly. I—I just… I don't know how to explain it." Lou couldn't quite put into words the feeling she'd had when Mia had walked away from her in the Pink Bean after she had invited her to Glow. It was a strange blend of pity, unexpected kindness, and an eagerness to understand.

"Please don't tell me you have the hots for her," Phil said.

Lou scoffed. "That would be ludicrous."

"Stranger things have happened."

"Who has the hots for whom?" Jared walked into the kitchen, followed by the twins—who were dressed in matching Spiderman pajamas and looked much too excited to be ready for bed.

"I sure hope Phil still has the hots for you," Lou said quickly. "You do look rather dashing in that suit."

Jared straightened his posture and fiddled with his tie. "Why, thank you, young lady. By the way, you must let us know how we can repay you. I can assure you tonight will not be a Netflix night for you. These two are beside themselves because you're here." He sighed.

"You know it's my pleasure." Lou glanced at the twins who were doing a silly dance around the kitchen. Every time she saw them the desire to have children of her own flared up inside of her. Because subconsciously—and perhaps cruelly—that had also been the rule she had measured Meredith against. Could this be a potential co-parent to her children? One glance at Meredith as she stood gesticulating while she talked into her phone and Lou had known enough.

"We'll see what you have to say about that when we get back and you're close to a nervous breakdown," Jared joked.

For the next hour, Lou didn't have a second of brainpower available to think about her conversation with Phil or Meredith's failed chances as she played with Toby and Yasmine. She finally got them into bed, read them the same story three times over, and they eventually fell asleep—suddenly and in the most outrageous position, the way only young children can.

It was only when she sat on the couch and poured herself the remainder of the bottle of wine Phil had opened that she had the chance to think and, immediately, her mind drifted toward Mia, as it had been doing a lot lately.

Lou was fairly certain she didn't have the hots for her, but she could not ignore Mia's presence on the outskirts of her life as easily as she had expected—or wanted.

---

The next Monday Lou and Amber were having lunch at Glow. Earlier, they'd had their daily cup of coffee and tea at the Pink Bean, and Amber had again showed a more courteous demeanor toward Mia.

"Do you think people can truly change?" Lou asked.

Amber smiled enigmatically. "Oh yes, but before I elaborate, may I inquire as to why you're asking me such a deep and philosophical question on an ordinary Monday?"

"I've noticed some change in your behavior when it comes to Mia lately." Lou knew she could be straightforward with Amber. "You seem to have warmed to her."

Amber pouted, which made her cheeks dimple. "Well, it's hard to give the cold shoulder to the person who tweaked our online ads so successfully."

"Of course. I get that."

"But?" Amber asked.

"That's my question. Do you think someone like Mia can truly change?"

Amber put down her fork and took a sip of water. "To be completely honest with you, if you hadn't told me about Mia, I would never have known. I'm not an expert on personality types and the traits that define a bully, but I would never in a million years have pegged Mia as one. I haven't spent a lot of time with her myself, but I know people who have, and for that reason I think Mia might actually have changed."

"Are you talking about Micky?"

"They have been spending quite a bit of time together, yes." Amber scrunched her lips together again. "You should talk to Micky."

"I should?" This took Lou aback.

"She knows Mia better. She might know… other things."

Lou's eyes grew wide. "Does Micky know about what happened with Mia and me?" Instant panic in her gut.

"I consider you a friend, Lou. As your friend, I'm telling you that you might benefit from a conversation with Micky. I'll also tell you that whatever Micky knows, she didn't get from me. Confidentiality is important to me." Only Amber could say such a thing in such a solemn tone of voice.

"So Mia told her?" Lou couldn't believe it. The nerve of Mia.

"None of this is for me to say. But to get back to your very first question. You and I are cut from the same cloth. That's one of the reasons I hired you. I saw a lot of myself in you. And I think that, if I can believe that a person can fundamentally change who they are, so can you. Not only that, though. I believe in the power of forgiveness. I think you do too. I know it sounds radical, perhaps foolish to your ears right at this very moment, but forgiveness sets you free. That's what I believe."

"You think I should forgive her?" Lou wondered if she had started this conversation because Amber would push her to think about Mia differently. Because she had seen with her own eyes how Amber had warmed to Mia, and it wasn't a fake business-like kind of warmth because Mia was helping her. It was more than that. Amber knew something. So did Micky. What on earth had Mia told Micky? Because those two were still chummy, getting chummier by the day, it seemed, and Micky didn't seem like the kind of person who would be easily fooled by Mia's smile and helpful behavior.

"No, Lou, that's not for me to say at all. But I can tell you that I was not always the person you see sitting in front of you today. I was once consumed by a different but equally destructive kind of rancor, because I felt I had been so wronged. But step by step, because of my practice, I was able to see things differently. It's not because some things are inexcusable that they can't be forgiven. Because by not forgiving someone, you're often harming yourself much more than the person needing to be forgiven."

"I would just really like to know what Mia has said to Micky." Lou knew there was no point in pressing Amber to tell her. If Micky had asked her to keep it from her, Amber would never violate that trust.

"Ask her." If Amber was imploring her to talk to Micky

in such a way, Lou could only conclude that whatever Micky had found out was something compelling enough to make Amber change her mind about Mia as a bully.

"I will," Lou said, putting it at the very top of her priority list.

## Chapter Sixteen

Sheryl and Kristin had visited Annie's Bookshop, had crunched their own set of numbers, done all the talking they needed and, quite possibly because of the time restraints Pages put on them, had given Mia the go-ahead to have an exploratory conversation with Annie. Mia had known Annie for a long time and was a loyal customer. Hopefully Annie would realize that Mia only had Annie's best interests at heart.

Unable to keep the news to herself, Mia had told Jo as soon as Kristin had okay'ed the operation. They'd never had that Save Annie's Bookshop Committee meeting they'd joked about. So far, it hadn't been necessary. If Mia could get Annie on board, it might not be. But before she went to see Annie, she wanted to get Lou's take on it. Lou had known Annie for much longer and, perhaps, had a different point of view to offer. She was a less business-minded person and would, Mia guessed, focus more on the direct consequences on Annie's life and wellbeing of what she was about to propose.

Mia waited impatiently for Lou to turn up at the Pink

Bean, which was an odd sensation. Usually, the thought of Lou walking in made her jumpy, made her retreat behind the hissing sounds of the milk steamer and the bulk of the coffee machine.

When she did finally arrive, at the exact time Mia had known she would on a Tuesday—Lou and Amber were like clockwork—Mia couldn't stifle a smile. She didn't think twice about how her smile could be interpreted. Whether Lou would take it as a sneer that wasn't one, or it would throw her back to when she was seventeen. Mia was too fired up by her plans to pay attention to any of that, and was ready to shed the cloak of extreme prudence she had donned around Lou for the past few weeks.

"Can I talk to you for a minute?" she asked, after having poured Lou a strong cup of coffee—she knew how she liked it by now, strong and black, just as Mia did. "It's about Annie's."

Lou responded almost like any other person would. Not like Mia's former victim, always something flighty about her, an invisible shield of caution drawn up around her. At the mention of Annie's name, Lou's face actually lit up a fraction.

They sat down and, for the shortest of instances, Mia's eyes were glued to the glossy skin of Lou's upper arm.

"The Pink Bean wants a Newtown location. Annie needs something to inject new life into her business," Mia heard herself say, although it felt entirely different to be explaining this to Lou than to her bosses or even to Jo. To talk to Lou in this manner, without their past standing between them, was liberating—perhaps even a touch exhilarating. Having to cower under Lou's glance every single day, having to express through her body language how sorry she was—because she wasn't allowed to say it in words—had been exhausting.

This conversation with Lou was the most relaxed interaction they'd had since Lou had confronted her. Therefore, Mia allowed her glance to drift to Lou's shoulder line a few times more, allowed herself to be astounded by the magic hue of her skin, by the sheer aliveness in her eyes that grew bolder as Mia reached the end of her pitch.

"You know Annie well. Do you think she would be interested?"

"It definitely beats having to sell, which she is seriously considering, even though it would break her heart." Lou's demeanor was much more at ease as well. As if the common goal that had sprouted between them had taken away most of the tension, at least as long as this conversation lasted—which was why Mia didn't want it to end. She hoped the Pink Bean wouldn't suddenly be flooded with customers and she would have to rush behind the counter to help out Jo. Sitting here with Lou, their minds churning over the same bits of information and working toward a common aim, made her feel better than she had in long, nervy, self-effacing weeks.

Then another idea hit Mia. "I'm going to have a chat with her very soon. Would you like to come?" Lou arched up her eyebrows. "Only if you think that would be a good idea, of course." Mia was sure that having Lou by her side would help to put Annie at ease, but she wasn't sure whether she wasn't also asking Lou to join her because this refreshing moment of détente between them felt so good.

"I do think it's a good idea. The whole thing is a stroke of brilliance." Lou looked Mia in the eye for a second, as if she was trying to find the old Mia in there, trying to gauge whether that younger version of Mia still existed.

"Thanks. It's really not that brilliant. It's pretty straightforward, actually."

"Don't be so humble, Mia," Lou said. "It really doesn't suit you." She flashed a smile.

Was she cracking jokes now? Mia smiled back. Maybe she should go to a yoga class one of these days. See what Lou was like in front of a bunch of people in downward-facing dog.

"Should we make an appointment or just stop by?" Mia asked.

"I'll call her," Lou said. "I think it better to not just barge in. And her wife, Jane, should probably be there as well."

"Okay. Thanks." Mia leaned back in her chair. "Any afternoon or evening this week is fine with me."

Lou looked as though she had just swallowed a joke. There was a glint of mischief in her eye that retreated as soon as it had shown up. "I'll let you know." She pushed her chair back. "Should I send you a message on Tinder or are you giving me your number?"

Mia suppressed a chuckle. "You'd have to swipe right first before you could message me on there." She looked around for a stray napkin, but couldn't find one.

"Ah, yes." Lou's relaxed, jokey mood seemed to be fading fast.

"Just a sec." Mia headed to the counter, found a piece of paper, and then proceeded to do something she had never believed would happen. She gave Louise Hamilton her number.

---

"It used to be that the bookshop was our livelihood and made up for the money I didn't earn with my books," Jane said. "These days, things are rather different."

All four of them were having coffee at The Larder and Mia was quickly realizing that the person she would be negotiating with would not necessarily be Annie, but Jane.

"Ironically, monthly digital book sales of Jane's books are

much higher than what we sell in the shop. We have so many authors on offer, but everyone wants to read on their Kindle or phone these days."

"Not everyone," Lou said. "I only ever read on paper."

"Paper books will always remain, but it's a reality that e-books are quickly catching up. I'm just as guilty as the next person. My wife runs a bookshop, yet I'm reading more and more on Kindle."

This sparked another idea in Mia's brain, but she would talk about what she had come here for first.

"I'm an all paper girl," Mia said.

"Oh, I know that," Annie said. "You must have quite the collection by now." She winked at Mia.

"I do. I love books and I love bookshops like yours. They offer something that the big chains can't. The number of books Annie has personally recommended to me, and the hours of joy she has provided me because of them. There's just something about the vibe of an indie store like Annie's. When you walk in, you immediately feel like you'll be taken care of. It's also a haven, a place away from modern technology. No phones, no tweets—only prose. I want this shop to go on forever." Mia threw in a smile. She glanced at Lou for a second and saw her looking back with an amused expression on her face.

"Your passion is admirable," Jane said. "And we feel exactly the way you do, but unfortunately not enough people have the same kind of passion for bookshops. They come in and run their fingers over the spines for the sensation of having an actual book in their hands, but nine times out of ten it's more an act of nostalgia than a reason to purchase. People don't buy anymore. Just the other week, we had a day with no sales. Zero. Nobody in Newtown needed a book that day. Isn't that sad?"

"Or they got it at Pages," Annie said wryly.

"Have you ever thought about serving coffee in the shop?" Mia cut straight to the chase.

Jane didn't seem the least bit surprised by this suggestion. "Of course we have. Everyone is doing it these days, but, in reality, it would be another investment in something we're not sure we can make work. Buy one of those expensive machines because no one would be caught dead anymore drinking a simple filter coffee, of course. Oh no. And Annie would be spending her time making coffee for people."

"It has never really been my goal in life," Annie said. "I know I'm a bit of a dreamer, and it's coming to catch up with me now, but I've always run the shop on expertise and careful curation. Up to five years ago, people actually came in to see what I had selected as book of the week, and they bought it. Books are my pride and joy. Fancy hot beverages not so much. And it's not as though I don't want to adapt to save the business, it's just that we've had to ask ourselves whether it would really be worth it, at our age, you know? I think we've come to the conclusion that it wouldn't. Not really."

"What if someone else took care of all of that for you?" Mia asked.

"How do you mean?" Annie asked.

"The coffee shop where I work in Darlinghurst, the Pink Bean, is looking to open a branch in Newtown. We thought about your shop. It could become a very appealing mixture of coffee shop and independent, curated bookshop. A destination, where one business feeds off the other."

Jane narrowed her eyes, but didn't immediately say anything. Annie straightened her posture, cocked her head, examined Mia's face. "Are you pulling our leg? Why would you make us such an offer? What's really in it for you?" She seemed to have her hackles up—perhaps because she had been made to listen to similar offers one time too many.

"What Mia is saying," Lou said, "is that we all want for this bookshop to stay in business."

"We? Who is this *we* you're talking about?" Jane's tone was milder, yet very inquisitive.

"All of us at the Pink Bean," Mia said.

"And me. And Mom and Dad. All your friends," Lou was quick to add.

"As for what's in it for the Pink Bean: a wonderful location that can be much more than just a coffee shop. Which is exactly what we're trying to make of the first Pink Bean as well. We're already doing evening events in that one. But this place offers a whole other set of possibilities. And, well, I probably don't need to tell you this." Mia held up her coffee cup. "Coffee sells. It's black gold. People spend much more on coffee than on books these days. In fact, they'd happily buy a latte with all the trimmings that is gone from their lives in a matter of minutes, than a book that will give them hours of reading pleasure. That's what the world is like these days."

"Don't I know it. Some of my e-books cost less than a cup of coffee, and people still have the audacity to complain that prices are too high," Jane said.

"It's all a matter of perception," Mia said. "But what if you could benefit from this, admittedly, somewhat skewed perception in people's minds?"

"How do you see this working in a practical sense?" Jane asked.

Mia explained the possibilities, which all came down to one thing: a shared space containing Annie's Bookshop and the second Pink Bean branch.

"Please feel free to think about this as long as you like. I will also happily put you in touch with the Pink Bean owners, Kristin and Sheryl. This was just an exploratory conversation, a pitch made by two friendly faces, although Kristin and Sheryl are plenty friendly themselves."

"And just so you know," Lou said, coming to Mia's rescue again, enhancing her presentation, "the Pink Bean is a gay-friendly place. It would mesh well with what you've always tried to do here. Because it always pisses me off when I do end up at Pages that they don't have an LGBT section. Not even in their big branch in the CBD. I think it's important."

"Because that's not where the money is," Jane said. "I should know."

Mia made a mental note to read one of Jane's books. She had seen them in the shop, but Annie—perhaps out of false modesty regarding her wife—had never recommended them.

"It's still important," Annie said. "I agree with you on that."

"Remember when you gave me *The Well of Loneliness* when I was eighteen?" Lou asked Annie. "That meant so much to me. Especially then."

"The good old days, when teenagers came to bookshops and accepted the owner's recommendations." She moved her hand across the table and cupped Lou's in hers. "Of course, you were always much more to me than just a teenager."

Mia tried to ignore the throwback to Lou's teenage years. She could only hope Lou had found some comfort in the books Annie had given her, not only regarding her burgeoning lesbianism, but also regarding other, more pressing and painful matters at the time.

"We certainly have a lot to think about," Jane said. "Thank you for the opportunity."

They said their goodbyes and when they stood outside Mia suddenly didn't know what to do. Should she ask Lou for a drink to discuss the meeting? They had taken a taxi from Darlinghurst earlier, but Mia was not going back in that direction.

"So you live near here?" Lou asked.

"Yes. Just a few blocks that way," she pointed to their left. "Very glamorously above a fish and chip shop."

"Really? That must be a temptation after you come home from a boozy night out."

Mia chuckled and before she had a chance to reply, Lou said, "I'd better go," and started looking around for a taxi.

"Thanks for doing this," Mia said, seeing the chance of asking Lou for a quick drink slip through her fingers. Perhaps it was too soon. Perhaps this was all she could ever hope for and there would always be a wall between them. "You know them best. Do you think they'll go for it?"

"I learned to stop predicting people's behavior and decisions a long time ago," Lou said matter-of-factly, and whether this was an intentional jibe at Mia or not, it still hit her straight in the gut. "We'll see."

A taxi pulled up, Lou gave her a quick wave good-bye, and disappeared into the falling darkness.

## Chapter Seventeen

The day after the meeting with Annie and Jane, after which Lou had dashed off in a taxi even though she might have said yes if Mia had asked her for a post-meeting drink, Lou asked Micky if they could have a private chat. If she'd had the opportunity to talk to Micky, and to find out what she knew about Mia that Lou didn't, she might have been inclined to hang out in Newtown longer last night, but she needed to know first. She needed to know now.

Between Lou's last afternoon class and her evening one, they ended up at a bar. Wine for Micky, sparkling water for Lou.

"I don't really know how to broach this topic," Lou said, "without just blurting it out." She couldn't quite meet Micky's gaze. There was something so vulnerable about making eye contact with someone of whom she suspected she knew all about what happened to her as a teenager. Lou had been uneasy around Micky since Amber had suggested Lou talk to her, and it had been surprisingly hard to bring herself to ask the question. But last night's stint in Newtown had urged her on. "I know Mia has told you something about our, er, past. And I would like to know what."

Instant pity in Micky's glance. Great. Lou was not after pity. She just wanted information.

Micky cleared her throat. "She told me she bullied you during your last year in high school. That there are no excuses for her behavior and that she's very ashamed of the person she was back then."

"That's it?" Lou could hardly believe that was all Micky knew. These were just the simple facts. This was not information Amber would urge her to obtain from Micky.

"That's all I can tell you," Micky said, "without breaking Mia's trust."

"But you understand the reasons why I would want to know?"

"Of course I do, Lou. And I want you to know. But she explicitly asked me not to tell you because she doesn't want her behavior to be excused. And she certainly doesn't want me to make excuses for her."

Lou scoffed. "That's because it can't be excused."

"I don't entirely agree." Micky sipped her wine. One sip clearly wasn't enough, because she quickly sipped again. "I don't want to underestimate your suffering and the impact of bullying. And I realize even having this conversation is like skating on thin ice, but I appreciate both you and Mia very much. You are two kind, considerate, thoughtful people with your heads screwed on right. Daughters any mother would be proud of. No matter what happened in the past." She paused. "It happened a long time ago, Lou. And the Mia you knew then, I dare to guess, is nothing like the person we've all gotten to know over the past few weeks."

"Oh yes, Mia the saint. The new girl on the block no one can get enough of or heap enough praise on. I'm starting to get sick of all of that."

"I understand that. I truly do. And I was shocked when Mia told me, but I was also surprised by her candor, by her willingness to tell me about that ugly part of her life, of herself. She was a teenager back then, just like you. Someone trying to come to grips with a life that was often hard."

"Yes, well, that's not really something I can take into consideration. What she did decimated me. Incapacitated me for too long, because even if it was only for a while in my teens, it was still too long for me. An entire school year, Micky. She waited for me for ten months. She went out of her way so she could bully me, call me names, make me feel so small I just wanted to disappear."

"I know. And I'm so sorry that happened to you. But that was a different Mia."

"I don't understand why she told you."

"She told me because I asked. Because it's so obvious that there is bad blood between you. Remember that night at Martha's when you and Amber tried to pretend she didn't exist? Amber tells me everything, and suddenly she was so harsh on Mia, telling me to not bring her into Glow anymore, even though she was helping us. That set off quite a few alarm bells. I asked Mia, and she told me. And I'm sorry that I can't tell you more, but I will tell you this: Mia has suffered too because of this. And I'm not saying you can compare the two, or that her suffering equals yours, because that's a losing game from the get-go if we're going to start comparing, but life is more complicated, and people are more complex than the mean teenagers we see them as sometimes."

"And what am I supposed to do with this information? Amber urged me to talk to you about this, but I'm really none the wiser."

Micky filled her cheeks with air, then let the air seep out

of her mouth slowly. "There's only one thing you can do, Lou." She tilted her head. "Talk to her about it."

"If only that wasn't the very last thing on my agenda."

"You've been getting on better lately, haven't you?"

"Getting on? I've been tolerating her because she's helping out my mother's friend." Lou finally looked Micky in the eye. "And you, us, the studio. But I don't want to talk to her. Not about any of that. We had our conversation. I confronted her. I can be civilized to her, but that's it."

"And that's the part I don't believe," Micky said. "We wouldn't be sitting here having this conversation if that was all you wanted. You wouldn't have talked to Amber about her if you didn't have an urge to truly put this behind you. I think the only way you can even begin to do so, now that you've come face-to-face with her again, is by having a conversation. Not a confrontation, but an open talk, where both parties get to say their piece."

Lou shook her head. "I'm not sure I can do that."

"But you can at least try." Micky was not letting Lou off the hook easily.

"It's good to know she has charmed you."

"She hasn't *charmed* me, Lou. She's just a genuinely nice person. And I truly believe that, even knowing what I do about her."

"I have to get ready for my next class," Lou said and rose. Deep down, she knew there was truth in what Micky had said, and if Mia truly had such good excuses for her past behavior, part of her was curious to learn all about them—if only to refute them. But the whole thing didn't sit right with her. She wanted to be reminded of that time as little as possible, and she was finally able to be around Mia without *only* thinking about that. Which was a big step forward already. She wasn't sure when she'd be ready for the next one, because this was beginning to feel like one step forward and two steps back.

---

The conversations she'd had with Micky and Amber kept stirring in Lou's mind. Pieces of them would catch her unawares while she was teaching or even just walking past the Pink Bean. Then there was the image of Mia herself that wouldn't leave her alone. Of present-day Mia, not the girl she once knew, but the woman who made her coffee and had come to Annie's rescue.

Lou was having breakfast at home. She had told her parents that Mia Miller was working at the Pink Bean, but she hadn't told them that it was Mia who had come up with the idea for the coffee/bookshop. She didn't talk about Mia much at all, except for the short announcement after spotting her at the Pink Bean for the first time, because it was not something she wanted to revisit with her parents. Not because they didn't care, but because they cared too much. Her father especially would want to have endless conversations about it, about how she felt now, and how she had dealt with the emotions of worthlessness over the years. He had a tendency to see her for a much more delicate person than she actually was. Lou had had to toughen up; she'd had no choice. And running to her daddy was no longer a tactic she wished to employ.

"Penny for your thoughts," her dad said. "You've been chewing on the same mouthful of granola for five minutes."

"Just some stuff going on at work," Lou said.

"Ah, I thought it was another date gone wrong." He flashed her a smile. Lou's mother had left for work already and it was just the two of them at the breakfast table.

Lou glanced at her father and realized that, despite her

wanting to spare him from her recent agony, he was probably the only person she could talk to about this. He knew and understood to an extent no one else could, because he had known Lou all her life, and he had been the one whose arms she had fled into when she was running away from Mia's taunts. He knew how sensitive she was. Not just because of what had happened to her, but by nature. He knew because he was her father.

When Lou was a teenager, on her worst days, it could hurt her so much that the color of her skin didn't match his, and she believed he couldn't possibly understand how she felt. Yet she had always turned to him more than to her mother, whose skin was a few shades darker than hers, and who took so much pride in being an Aboriginal person. Lou could never reconcile the fierceness of her mother's pride with the insults Mia Miller threw at her.

Yet, she didn't say anything to her father. Partly because she didn't even know where to start, and partly because she didn't want him to worry about her the way he always did—she was thirty-two, for heaven's sake. But mostly because Micky had been right. In her heart, she knew that the only way to find out was to ask Mia. Ask her what had made her say the things she had said, again and again.

"I haven't been on any more dates, Dad." She quickly spooned up the rest of her breakfast. "You'll be the first to know when I do. Fathers have a right to know these things about their grown-up daughters," she joked.

Her father didn't smile. "I'm just worried about you."

Ah, there it was. When Lou had moved to Brisbane to get away from her life in Sydney and start over, she had also taken advantage of the opportunity to escape her parents' over-protectiveness. They'd meant well, but to put herself together again she'd had to do it without them. She had missed them terribly, and spent hours on the phone with them every week, but at the time, it felt like the only way forward.

"I can take care of myself these days."

"I know you can, but I'm still allowed to worry."

"I have to go." Lou checked her watch ostentatiously. "See you tonight."

She gave him a quick wave and left her worried father to clean up the breakfast table.

———

"Can we talk?" Lou asked Mia as soon as she entered the Pink Bean. She no longer needed Amber's presence next to her to go up to the counter and order a coffee from Mia— and Mia no longer hid in a corner when she saw her approach.

"Now?" Mia asked, her body having gone stiff a little.

"After your shift, if you have time."

"Lunch?" Mia consulted her watch. "I'll be done in half an hour."

"Just a quick chat is fine." Lou didn't want to go as far as to have lunch with Mia. Besides, the conversation she wanted to have would only be made harder if they had to chew food in between. "In private." Lou had considered asking Mia to her parents' house for privacy reasons, but she didn't want to invite her into her home. It was a step too far. "I'll wait for you."

"Okay, sure." Mia gave her a half-smile. "Care to tell me what it's about?" She was growing bolder around Lou, less on guard—less as if she was still punishing herself.

"Not now." Lou said in a tone that she hoped would convey what it was about. She had no doubt Mia would understand. Because it was the one big thing between them everything still flowed back to. Truth be told, Lou was ready for that to be over. Maybe Micky had been right in more ways than one.

"Okay." Mia handed Lou her coffee. "I'll come and find you."

Lou found a spot in the corner by the window, so she could look out over the street and rehearse what she was going to say. But as she sat there, she found her eyes drawn back to the counter, where Mia was bantering with Jo, or joking with customers, just being her jolly self—the one she had become later in life.

Lou quickly gave up staring out of the window and pretended to read, watching Mia from under her lashes. There was a gracefulness about her that could only be described as effortless. When you looked at Mia you could tell she was one of those people who didn't care much about what others thought of them, someone with confidence to spare, not the kind that bordered on arrogance, but the kind that came with simply being okay with herself.

It had been that exact attitude that had ticked off Lou so much when she'd first seen Mia turn up at the Pink Bean. It didn't matter that their troubles had happened fifteen years ago. How dare this woman walk around with such a self-assured gait, such a charismatic smile, such a jokey way with everyone who crossed her path?

Now, Lou saw it in a different light. When she set her own grievances aside, and saw Mia as just another Pink Bean patron, she understood why she'd heard a customer flirt with Mia uncontrollably once, even though there were people in the line behind her. Mia's open demeanor invited that kind of behavior. She had a flirty smile. She had the clear eyes and straight-toothed kind of grin that made people warm to her easily. Even Lou was beginning to.

When Mia had flirted with Lou right after they'd met, perhaps, if they had been complete strangers, Lou might have flirted back. That was the kind of person Mia was. And that was also why all the others couldn't help but sing her praises, even Micky, who knew all about Mia's past. Even Amber, who strongly believed people could change for the better. Leaving only Lou behind with her grudge to hold.

Mia was walking toward her now. It had only been ten minutes since their conversation but she'd probably struck a deal with Josephine. She was the Pink Bean golden child now, she could get away with anything.

"I'm all ears." Mia put her hands on the back of a chair, waiting for Lou's okay to sit.

"Care for a walk?" Lou asked.

"Sure."

They were escorted out of the Pink Bean by a wave from Jo, then they stood on the sidewalk. It was up to Lou to determine the route and to raise the subject she wanted to talk about.

She started walking, with no destination in mind, although she would have preferred to have this conversation in private. Her house was empty. Both her parents were at work. Could she bring Mia Miller into her safe haven, even though she had already decided she didn't want her there? As the moment of having to ask questions neared, and nerves started manifesting themselves, Lou felt like she didn't have much choice. She was the one who couldn't ask this question of Mia in the street, and who needed the protection of four walls around her. Besides, walking around in Darlinghurst, where they both knew a lot of people, could never be private enough.

"Let's go to my house," Lou said. "Well, my parents' house to be exact. And before you say anything, yes, I am part of the trend of people in their thirties returning home to live with their parents."

"I'm not saying a word," Mia joked, her tone tense.

They walked in silence, with long, determined strides. Lou let them in and they sat in the lounge. It was so silent around them when they sat down that Lou heard Mia's stomach growl.

"Looks like you're hungry."

"I tend to skip breakfast when I have to get up early. We were slammed today so I didn't get a chance to have a quick bite in between."

"I can make you a sandwich later," Lou said, even though she wasn't sure what *later* entailed exactly, or whether she would still want to be around Mia, let alone offer to make her a sandwich.

"It's fine." Mia shuffled in her seat.

"I had a chat with Micky," Lou began. "Well, I had a chat with Amber first, then with Micky." Argh, the words were coming out all jumbled again. She wished she had some of Mia's suaveness. "Amber told me to talk to Micky, then Micky told me to talk to you. Apparently, you confided in her."

"I didn't mean to, Lou. Believe me, I don't go around talking to new friends about what a horrible person I used to be. We had a few drinks and Micky isn't stupid. She had sussed something out. It was either that or lie to her face."

"I don't mind that you told her. I would just really like to know what it was exactly that you said to her." To her surprise, Lou managed to keep her voice steady.

Mia rested her elbows on her knees and buried her face in her hands for a few seconds. When she looked up again, her eyes were red-rimmed, and she looked a whole lot less confident. "Are you sure you want to hear this?"

"Yes." Lou nodded to add more force to her words.

"I, er, I told her about how I grew up. About the kind of man my father was." She averted her gaze. "Which I don't want to use as an excuse. And I said the same thing to Micky.

I'm not looking to be excused. All I'm looking for are ways to live with what I've done."

"What kind of man was he?" Lou thought back to the conversation she'd had with her father only this morning. She figured that, unlike hers, Mia's dad was not a kind-hearted, overly protective man whom Mia could confide in about pretty much anything.

"A bitter racist. A bully to my mother. Someone so disappointed with life, he tried to suck the joy out of it for all of us as well." Her voice had stopped trembling. "He was—well, *is* an awful man. And, sadly, a man I allowed myself to be influenced by for too long." She sighed. "All the words I used to shout at you, I learned from him." She buried her head in her hands again. When she glanced up, she said, "I should have known better. I did, in fact, know better. Of course, I did. Your tears told me enough. Told me that what I was doing was wrong, but I grew addicted to the power of my words. To the power I could wield over someone else, someone with a different skin color to me, because, in the process, I could try and make my dad proud as well." She wiped a sudden tear from her cheek. "I'm so sorry, Lou. It was all just such a fucking mess back then, my entire life was like walking this tightrope between feeling powerless at home and this constructed, false sense of power at school. Because I had a big mouth, and I could at least use that to my advantage."

Lou didn't know what to say, so she just kept quiet. Of course Micky would feel sorry for Mia after she told her a sob story like that, but it was different for Lou, who had been on the receiving end of Mia's anger and frustration for far too long.

"I wish I could somehow prove to you that I'm not an inherently mean person. I'm not like my father. In fact, I haven't seen him in more than ten years. I want nothing to do with him. I know what I did was wrong, and I will carry that guilt with me for the rest of my life, but I had to get on with my life as well. I had to find a way to make it work knowing what I had done to you and others. Knowing that I had let my father's hatred seep into my psyche and wreak the havoc it did. I walked away from him and never looked back."

"I don't know what to say to that or how to react." Lou felt numb, like the part of her brain responsible for telegraphing emotions had been turned off.

"You don't have to say anything. But you asked, so I told you. This is what I told Micky, who was surprisingly understanding."

"What did she say?"

"I, er, I don't feel comfortable repeating her words."

"Oh, for crying out loud. Just tell me." Lou was surprised by the vehemence in her own voice. "First Micky doesn't want to tell me what you said, now you don't want to tell me what she said. That's all well and good, if only I wasn't caught dead in the middle of it all." She shook her head.

"Okay." Mia nodded. "She said I was just a kid back then. A troubled kid who made a mistake. It happened fifteen years ago and despite the severity of bullying, I, er, I guess I should forgive myself. Something like that. I'm paraphrasing."

"And *have* you forgiven yourself?" Lou asked, hearing echoes of Amber's words about how forgiveness is the only way forward. "And do you expect me to forgive you as well?"

"I will never forgive myself. But I have allowed myself to move on. To live a life I can be proud of, be someone I can be proud of. And no, I would never ask for your forgiveness. I would never ask you for anything."

Lou glanced at Mia. All the things she had thought about her before, about how confident and charismatic she was, had been stripped away. This was yet another version of Mia. The one who looked as decimated as Lou had felt fifteen years ago.

"I'm glad you told me," she said.

"Thanks for asking." Mia appeared so distraught, Lou had to suppress to urge to sit next to her and throw a comforting arm around her shoulder. The thought dawned on her that, perhaps, she had started forgiving Mia already. Maybe she had started after seeing Mia's tears at Glow that night, the obvious anguish on her face at being confronted with her former self. Or when she'd walked away from her at the Pink Bean after Lou had invited her to come to yoga. Or when she'd been pleading her case to Annie and Jane, so alive and in her element. Or simply when she'd been looking at her while Mia was at work in the Pink Bean, like she had done so earlier. The Mia who didn't know Lou was watching. The unencumbered, free person Lou had taken such offense to and who was the polar opposite of the person sitting across from her right now.

"I truly do think you should come to yoga some time." It was all Lou could think of to say. It was an invitation that held much more meaning than the permission it gave, and she could only hope Mia would see that. "It has helped me so much to just… be at peace with myself, if even for an hour a day."

"An hour a day is quite a long time." Mia brushed some more tears from her cheek and the beginnings of a smile started to form on her lips. "That's quite a promise to make."

"It's not a promise. Yoga is not some miracle bestowed upon the western world to feel better about ourselves just because we take to the mat once a day. It takes time and work and consistency."

"I'm glad it helped you. And that you found a job you're so passionate about."

In that moment, Lou was just glad she had changed the topic of conversation. If they'd kept rehashing the past in such an intense manner, she might have ended up crying alongside Mia.

"How about that sandwich now?" She stood, and took a pace in the direction of the kitchen.

"I'm not very hungry anymore," Mia said.

## Chapter Eighteen

After Lou had asked twice, Mia took it as an order to attend one of Lou's classes—or as part of her still-ongoing penance, perhaps.

So there she stood, her shoulders screaming because of the downward-facing dog Lou had had them in for the past half hour, or so it seemed.

"Spread out your weight more." Lou spent as much time walking among her students as she spent at the front of the class and it was the second time she had stopped next to Mia to correct her posture. "It will hurt less." She wasn't shy about touching Mia either, and put a hand on the small of her back to coax her into a more balanced pose.

God, this was so strange. This was supposed to be a beginners class, but because yoga was so new to her, Mia couldn't quite keep up with the flow and needed the occasional break. In those moments she couldn't stop thinking about the strange twist of fate that had made her end up in a Louise Hamilton yoga class.

Had it only been two days ago that she'd sat crying in the couch at Lou's home? Such a cathartic moment if ever there was one. Hard and confrontational as it had been at the time, afterwards, she'd felt relieved. Because one less secret stood between her and Lou now. And it wasn't resolution or even a sense of having unburdened herself, just the feeling that something significant had happened on the path to truly forgiving herself. Mia might have said that she would never forgive herself, but before seeing Lou again she had believed that she had already done so. The truth most likely lay somewhere in between. In order to truly move on, she would need to forgive herself, but she would need Lou's forgiveness first to make that happen. Which made them unlikely co-travelers on this path. And which was why Mia had come to this yoga class—a class she had been banned from earlier.

At the same time, Lou was different and also very much like the person Mia had got to know when she stood in front of the room. There was a poise and elegance about her that Mia hadn't really seen in her before, but there was also the warmth in her tone of voice, the gentle insistence she put in it to guide, not push, her students to a higher level of understanding of this practice she spoke so passionately about.

Even though Lou had treated her cold-heartedly, there had always been a sense that that kind of coldness was alien to her, that she had to put on a mask to be so harsh, retreat into a former version of herself—a version she only was in front of Mia.

This yoga studio was where Lou was at her best, where she shone and guided newbies like Mia into, at the very least, getting a sense of what yoga could be.

"One last sun salutation," Lou said.

Mia had to glance at Micky next to her to get the order of the movements right.

"Don't look at what anyone else is doing," Lou said.

Did she have her eye on Mia? Did she see her cast her glance aside?

"Look at me." Lou went to her mat in the front of the room and effortlessly stepped into a lunge.

Mia did as she was told and fixed her gaze on Lou, with her high pony tail and the beige tank top she wore contrasting so deliciously with the darker color of her skin. She caught herself in the middle of the thought and refocused her attention on getting the pose right. Stepping back into a plank she could do; it was the jumping forward bit with two feet that came after downward dog that had been troubling her throughout.

They finished their last sun salutation of the class and were then instructed to lie down on their backs.

"Focus on the breath," Lou said, her voice so calm and steady, Mia wanted to record it so she could listen to it again later, when she was feeling flustered or overwhelmed. "You did a wonderful job today. You gave your body the gift of starting or deepening your practice. You did yourself a huge favor."

Mia had her eyes closed and she couldn't help but wonder if Lou was still watching her, even though she couldn't make many mistakes with the pose she was in now. How relaxing to just lie there, with Lou's pleasant voice washing over her, after having done this class, which wasn't so much about starting a practice for Mia, but about taking the outstretched hand that Lou had offered her.

"Great job everyone. Thank you for coming," Lou said after they'd all sat up and intoned a solemn *namaste* together.

When Mia went to drop off her mat by the door, where Lou was standing, she shot her a smile.

"Good job," Lou said, and Mia could tell that she meant it. "You should come again."

"Maybe I will." She shot Lou a different kind of smile now, a more audacious one.

"God, I'm so glad the two of you are talking." Micky had

sidled up to them. "The tension was starting to do my head in." She cocked her head at Mia. "I know it's against the spirit of yoga and all that, but this one is going to need some serious limbering up."

"You're not supposed to watch others while you're practicing," Mia was quick to say.

"I didn't need to watch. I heard you grunt all the way through." Micky flashed her a smile. "Is this a good time to invite you both to our house for Robin's birthday next Saturday? Or are we not there yet?"

"Depends," Lou said. "Will Meredith be there?"

"Yes, she will, but I'll tell her to keep well away and not accost you or harass you or re-swipe right on you in any way."

This made both Lou and Mia chuckle.

"I just don't want any drama," Lou said.

"Is that a yes?" Micky asked.

Mia nodded, then so did Lou.

---

After showering and saying good-bye to Micky, Mia waited for Lou outside Glow. She kept an eye on the bus stop, where her bus was supposed to arrive any minute, but after switching her phone back on after class, she'd found a message from Kristin on her phone about Annie and Jane.

Still in her yoga gear, Lou turned up a few minutes later. "You're still here," she said, surprised.

"I thought you might like to know that Kristin and I are going to Newtown tomorrow for a meeting with Annie and Jane. From what I gather, it might be a very productive, positive kind of meeting."

"They said yes?" There was genuine glee in Lou's tone.

"Not just yet, but I think we're on the right path. I'll keep you posted." Mia saw her bus round the corner. She glanced at it. There was no one else at the stop and if she didn't leave now to signal the driver, it would cruise right past.

"Thanks. And thanks for coming," Lou said. "Don't mind Micky. You know what she's like." She threw in a smile.

"Ah, shoot." Mia had been unable to tear herself away from Lou. "There goes my ride." The bus thundered past them.

"Do you have to wait long for the next one?"

"Twenty minutes if I'm lucky. It's all right."

"Your life will be so much easier once Annie and Jane say yes. No more commutes." Lou scrunched her lips together. "I was going home to take a nice long bath, but I can keep you company, if you like," Lou said. "As long as we don't go anywhere fancy, because I'm not exactly dressed for it."

*You look just fine to me*, Mia wanted to say, but wisely swallowed her words. "You don't have to. Wait with me, I mean."

"I know I don't have to, Mia."

The way she said it made Mia feel they'd taken another few steps on that road they were on together.

"Then I will gladly accept your offer. A quick drink at Grape Therapy?"

"Lead the way." Lou sent her a smile.

A couple of minutes later they both sat with a large glass of wine in front of them, and Mia was pretty sure she would miss her next bus as well. She didn't mind one bit.

"We'd best start thinking about Robin's birthday gift," Lou said.

Mia nodded. "Have you heard anything from Meredith?"

"Nope. Your Pink Bean scare tactics really worked." She grinned at Mia over her glass of wine.

"I didn't mean to overstep my bounds." Mia grinned

back. "But I can be on bodyguard duty again if you want me to."

"As I said, I can take care of myself these days."

Even though they were having an impromptu drink together, a lot of the things that were said between them harked back to the reason they knew each other. Mia guessed that wouldn't go away any time soon, or ever.

"Sheryl questioned me the other day about why you and I didn't get on," Mia said.

"Since starting work at Glow, I've also learned that some businesses in Darlinghurst really don't keep up a dividing wall between work and private life." Lou snickered.

"Yeah, and it's as if they can't stand it when two people who are new to the group and the neighborhood and the business don't get on. Like they take it as a personal fault or something."

"Or they're just really nosy." Lou sipped from her wine. "Although in Amber's case, I know she was genuinely just worried about me."

"They're a fun group. Very much up in each other's business, but kind at heart," Mia said. "I'm glad to know them." Mia would miss her morning shifts alongside Jo. Or perhaps she could persuade her to work in the Newtown branch with her, though she doubted Kristin would agree.

"Thanks for, huh…" Mia felt like she should say something, but she didn't know what. "…waiting with me. I think another bus just went past." What she actually meant to thank Lou for was for taking the first step. For reaching out to her, asking her to come to yoga, and treating her like a normal human being.

## Chapter Nineteen

As usual, Lou woke before her alarm clock, but today, she wanted to huddle under the covers and keep sleeping. She'd had a very pleasant dream she wanted to catch the tail end of. One of those dreams that left her feeling so satisfied and sensual and pleased with herself she never wanted to wake up from it, even though she couldn't remember the actual contents of it.

She turned on her side and rolled into a ball, scrunching her eyes shut, hoping the images and emotions she had been basking in would return to her, gather her in their loving arms again, and make her feel desired and taken care of.

Her eyes started fluttering open of their own accord, however, and she knew there was no use in trying to fall back asleep, even though she had woken up in the middle of a dream cycle. Instead, she switched off her alarm and tried to clear her head, hoping she could put a face to the person she had dreamed of and who had made her feel so spectacular—much better than she'd felt in real life for a very long time.

She focused on her breath and tried to empty her mind, something she often coaxed her students to try, but was so notoriously difficult because there was always some trailing thought or wandering notion to bother yourself with.

She couldn't even conjure up what the dream person had done exactly to make her feel so good, to make her want to stay in bed, go back to sleep, and experience it all over again. Had it been an erotic dream? Lou couldn't even be certain of that, even though she felt a certain degree of arousal hum in her blood. It was more a sense of utter well-being that had washed over her. Complete contentment and peace with herself. And someone else had been involved, of that she was sure.

But it was the nature of dreams to be fleeting, to sometimes leave you wanting more, and often, leave you wondering what they meant and what your subconscious was trying to tell you. Either way, Lou soon realized she wasn't going to find out more about this dream, no matter how much she wanted to return to it. It was time to let it go and get up.

It was Saturday morning and she had three classes to teach, of which two were back-to-back. Then, tonight, she had a party to attend. Truth be told, she was a little worried about Meredith being there. Everyone she'd gotten to know over the past few months would be there. It would be a celebration of one of Meredith's friends. Surely she would be in no mood to create a scene. With that thought, Lou stretched, got out of bed, and started her day.

---

The first person Lou saw after Micky showed her in was Meredith. They caught each other's glance and Lou thought it only polite to send her a quick smile. After all, the woman had never done anything truly bad to her; she'd just been a bit pushy, which Lou chose to see as flattery.

It was only after Meredith smiled back at her, and Lou could only decipher that smile as weirdly triumphant, that she noticed Meredith had not come to the party alone. She had a woman on her arm who was clearly more than a friend or colleague.

*Good for her*, Lou thought, and started mingling. Micky's living room seemed filled to the brim already, all the couches and chairs were taken and a bunch of people stood around the dining table.

Lou never felt comfortable in situations like this so, after wishing Robin a happy birthday, she went to find Amber, who was chatting with Caitlin and Sheryl. She glanced around but didn't see Mia. Was she now actively looking forward to when Mia Miller would arrive?

"Good news, Lou," Sheryl said. "It looks like we'll come to an agreement with Annie and Jane next week."

"That's great." Lou knew this already, but didn't want to spoil Sheryl's glee. Two days ago, Annie had called her and asked Lou, one old friend to another, to vouch for Kristin and Sheryl's character.

The only negative thing Lou had been able to think of was that they had hired Mia, although she had soon corrected her thought—and had certainly not voiced it to Annie, because it was Mia who had set the whole thing in motion.

Sheryl raised her glass. "To the second location of the Pink Bean."

They all clinked their glasses together.

"Well, it's not going to be there tomorrow, but it's going to be wonderful once it is." Sheryl peered at Lou. "That Jane is a feisty one. I like her."

"At first, I couldn't believe it was Jane Quinn you were talking about," Amber said.

"Are you keen on reading some spicy lesbian romance then?" Caitlin said in a teasing tone.

"Aren't *you*?" Amber retorted. "Or is that not intellectual enough for you?"

"I've read a few," Caitlin admitted.

"I haven't," Sheryl said, "but I've bought a couple and I will rectify the situation as soon as possible." Sheryl looked at Lou again.

"I couldn't possibly read any of her books. Annie is a friend of my mother's. It's just all too… weird for me."

"Oh come on, Lou," Caitlin said. "You're missing out. Put that thought out of your head at once."

"I can't. She's like an aunt to me. It's simply impossible."

They all chuckled.

"Ah, Mia, tell us, have you read any of Jane Quinn's books?"

Lou had taken her eye off the hallway entrance and hadn't seen Mia arrive.

"I tried," Mia said. "I really did, but I've known Annie for such a long time and I kept seeing her as one of the characters and I just couldn't get over that. It was awkward when I went back to the shop, you know." She smiled at Lou; Lou smiled back.

"So what are you saying?" Sheryl said, on a roll as usual. "If I were to write a lesbian romance, you would refuse to read it because you'd mistakenly cast me and Kristin in the roles of the characters? That's just ridiculous. Where's your imagination?"

"I just gave them almost the same reason, on account of Annie being a long-time family friend," Lou said to Mia. "They refuse to accept it, even though Sheryl has the audacity to judge us without having read any of the books herself. I think she believes romance to be beneath her."

Mia's eyes narrowed. Perhaps she wasn't expecting Lou

to give Sheryl lip like that. Lou hadn't been expecting it either, but this group of people just made her feel good about herself—made her able to be herself around them. And then, with Mia's narrowed eyes on her, with her smile crooked like that, and her dark hair falling into her eyes, and her hand quickly swooping it away, a flash of the dream she'd had last night came back to her. The other person in the dream who had made her feel so good. It was Mia. Lou quickly took a few sips from her drink to wash away the unsettling feeling that came over her.

Mia looked away, and said to Sheryl, "I would read every word of romance you ever write without qualms, boss. Just make sure none of your characters wear vests every day."

Everyone burst out laughing again, and Lou forgot about the dream, until the group dispersed and she found herself alone with Mia, hovering over the part of the table with the vegan snacks.

"I see Meredith has moved on," Mia said.

"Looks like it, which means you're off bodyguard duty." Her arm bumped lightly into Mia's and a flash of the dream came back to her—or was she making things up now? Mia's face as it leaned in toward her, ready to kiss her. "I'm surprised she even made it here. She'll probably get a call from work in ten minutes, leaving another poor woman disillusioned."

"Is that what happened on the date?"

"Yes, on a Sunday evening." Lou still couldn't keep the indignation about that out of her voice. "I'm sorry. I'm truly not that upset about Meredith, it's more that her actions evoked strong feelings about my ex and why we split."

"Not enough time for you?"

"Not just me. For herself either." Lou drank again. "But I don't really want to talk about my ex. I'm at a party. I'd rather enjoy myself."

"Anything I can do to enhance your enjoyment?" Mia's bare arm slid against hers again. Was it the effects of the three glasses of wine Lou had knocked back in quick succession or was it still the dream that was haunting her? Lou felt something warm and fuzzy come to life in the pit of her stomach.

"Yeah, tell me something, Mia Miller." Oh, it was definitely the alcohol. She should have one of those snacks soon. "How come you're single? I've witnessed Daisy shamelessly flirt with you more than once at the Pink Bean. Objectively speaking, you're a good-looking woman. And everyone here speaks so highly of you."

"Objectively speaking, huh?" Mia said with a smile on her face. "I'm not really looking, you know. What's wrong with being single?"

"There's nothing wrong with it, but then it does make me wonder why, if you're not looking, you're on Tinder."

Mia shook her head. "You got me." She shrugged. "A friend of mine set it up for me when I was having a bad day. I flipped through some profiles."

"All left swipes?" Lou inquired. "Nobody tickled your fancy at all?" Was she flirting? She'd better get herself in check.

"I wouldn't say nobody." Mia cocked her head.

"Pity you didn't take a chance on Meredith. She literally told me she swiped right on you and she could only conclude you'd swiped left."

"She told you?" Mia gave a chuckle. "Well, looks like I'm too late now." They both glanced at Meredith who was engaged in a too passionate display of public affection.

"And I was only her consolation prize after you didn't bite." Lou drank again. Tomorrow was Sunday. She was having fun—and an actual conversation with Mia Miller full of innuendo. A conversation she would otherwise be too uptight to have, but this was a party. And who said Lou couldn't party? Angie could say those things about Lou all she wanted—and it was true that Lou was usually the one who wanted to go home first when they were out together—but tonight, Lou was unattached, and in the company of new friends, and she quite liked the new life she was starting to build around them.

"You did say that I was *objectively* pretty." Mia angled her body more toward Lou, and Lou didn't feel any inclination to flinch away from her. "Could you possibly try to clarify that for me?"

Lou pouted and tried to think of how to get herself out of this. "It means that I think you have the kind of face that a lot of people would automatically swipe right on. Very symmetrical. Good teeth. I don't know, you have that wholesome look about you that a lot of people find attractive." Oh Christ, she was only digging herself in deeper.

Mia chuckled. "You might as well have said I look bland."

"No, bland is definitely not it." Lou pretended to give Mia a thorough once-over. "Maybe it's your hair. It just falls really nicely and it looks like it does of its own accord. It projects a kind of ease, and so does your body language."

"Holy moly, have I just gone into therapy without knowing?" Mia asked. "On Tinder, no one would have a clue about my body language."

"Of course they would. The way you hold yourself in the picture. The smile. That's all part of it."

"You sound like an expert."

"Hey girls. Do you need a refill?" They both held out their glass eagerly. "The cake will be out soon. Get ready to sing 'Happy Birthday'." She winked at them both, then went about refilling a few other guests' glasses.

"In my line of work, I get to observe a lot of people."

Lou tried to pick up the thread of their conversation again to defend herself. "I find body language fascinating." Lou was beginning to think of Mia as fascinating as well. She sipped from her freshly refilled glass. That dream was still doing her head in.

A hush traveled through the small crowd gathered in Micky's living room. Amber exited the kitchen with a chocolate cake chock-full of candles. A few people started singing "Happy Birthday" and Lou and Mia joined in. A round of applause followed for the birthday girl, followed by a short speech in slurred words thanking everyone for coming and urging them to stay for a good while longer and be merry.

In the hustle and bustle of the singing and cake distribution, Lou had gotten separated from Mia, who was now talking to Kristin. Lou was tipsy enough to talk to just about anyone right now, but when she saw Amber, she naturally gravitated toward her.

"You and Mia looked pretty chummy just now," Amber whispered in her ear. This sounded like something so unlikely for Amber to say, Lou cast a long, thorough glance into her boss's eyes. Dilated pupils. Watery gaze. She'd never thought she'd see the day, but Amber was just as far gone as the rest of them. It was that kind of party.

"Yes, well, isn't it better like this?" Lou asked, not expecting an answer, saying it more to herself than as a reply to Amber. Because it *was* infinitely better this way.

Amber held out her glass of wine and Lou clinked hers against it. Maybe she only felt this way because she had drunk too much, but even if that was the case, she wanted to enjoy the feeling of a heart free of grudges and animosity for as long as she could.

When people were starting to leave and the group dwindled down to about a dozen, Lou thought it a good idea to go home.

"Afterparty at my place," Amber shouted, after which Martha threw an arm around her and guided her to the couch while hushing her.

"I hope not." Mia had walked up to Lou. "I'm bone tired."

"Thank goodness we haven't started doing classes on Sunday yet. I've never seen her like this."

"Everybody needs to let their hair down." Mia shot her one of her smiles.

A commercial smile, that's what it was, Lou thought. She wasn't Amber-level drunk, but a good few of her inhibitions were lowered, to the point that she found herself turning to Mia fully, looking her in the eye, and asking, "Do you want to go out some time?"

Mia narrowed her eyes. She barely smiled, yet her entire face lit up. "How about I walk you home instead? Make sure you get there in one piece."

"Is that a *no*?"

Mia shook her head. "It's an ask-me-again-when-you're-sober." She put an arm on Lou's shoulder. "Okay?"

"I'm really not that drunk." Lou leaned into Mia slightly. "And don't you have a bus to catch?"

"I'm staying at Kristin and Sheryl's. Come on." She took her by the hand and walked her home.

## Chapter Twenty

Mia woke in Kristin and Sheryl's guest room, which was about the size of her entire studio in Newtown. The first thing she thought about was Lou. Clearly Lou had asked her out because she was drunk, and Mia was pretty sure the invitation wouldn't hold in the cold, sober light of day. Still, she couldn't help but feel a little smug about it.

She got up and found both of her hosts already sitting at the breakfast table. They both looked much more chipper than Mia felt. She hadn't been as wasted as Amber or Lou, but she'd had her fair share. She wondered how Lou would describe her if she saw her now.

"Good morning." Sheryl pulled a chair back for her. "Sleep well?"

"Very well. I could easily live in that room. It's beautiful and so big and it has its own bathroom. What more can a girl ask for?"

"You're welcome to stay here whenever you want. Call it a special Pink Bean employee perk," Kristin said and, without asking, poured her some coffee. She knew Mia took it black and strong.

"It's cheaper than giving you a company car," Sheryl said. "And we definitely want to keep you, so we must keep you happy." She winked at Mia.

"Seriously, Mia." Kristin sounded as if she meant it. "The room is yours whenever you need it."

"Thank you so much." Mia would definitely take them up on the offer. The number of times she had just missed a bus, arrived home late, and ended up having a quick meal at the fish and chip shop below. "An hour of extra sleep in the morning will do wonders for my performance at work." She smiled widely at them. Then her phone beeped.

The message was from Lou and it just read: *Ouch*.

Mia chuckled. "Someone's having a rough morning." She showed Kristin and Sheryl her phone screen.

"From Lou?" Sheryl asked. "You two seemed to be getting along well last night." Of course Sheryl would have noticed.

"Let's just say we set aside some of our differences. And Lou was pretty far gone." She hesitated for a second, wondering if she should confide in her employers, even though the fact that she was sitting at their Sunday breakfast table clearly meant they were becoming friends. "She even asked me out."

"She did?" There was genuine surprise in Kristin's voice.

"I told her to ask me again when she was sober." If Mia wanted advice on how to proceed next, she knew she would get a much more straight-forward answer from Sheryl than from Kristin. "I'm not even sure she will remember," Mia said.

"She texted you. She remembers," Sheryl said.

"Do you like her?" Kristin asked.

"Things are a bit, er, complicated between us."

"So I've noticed." Mia hadn't expected such a sharp reply from Kristin. Maybe she had a headache as well.

"I do… like her," Mia admitted. She remembered the flirty conversation they'd had last night. In fact, she'd run it through her head several times during the night.

"Then you should probably reply something," Sheryl said.

Mia saw them exchange a glance.

"Things like this excite Sheryl a great deal," Kristin said. "Please excuse her."

"What's more exciting than budding love?" Sheryl exclaimed.

"I wouldn't exactly call it that," Mia said.

"You're getting carried away, babe," Kristin said in her stern voice.

Mia studied her phone. She should reply. She was eager to find out if Lou still wanted to go out with her. If the offer still stood, she would give her a resounding yes.

She texted back: *Do you need me to bring you some pain killers?*

Not even a minute later, the reply came in: *Can we meet some time today? I would like to apologize in person.*

Mia didn't know what Lou would need to apologize for. They agreed to meet at the Pink Bean a few hours later. She summarized her text conversation for Kristin and Sheryl.

"Ah, a first date at the Pink Bean. That's truly the reason we wanted a coffee shop. We've done a pretty good job of it so far." She smirked at Mia. Kirstin shook her head.

———

Mia had borrowed one of the Jane Quinn books Sheryl had recently bought and sat reading, waiting for Lou to arrive. She saw her scuttle past the big window before she entered the Pink Bean, head held down, as though she had engaged in the most shameful activities last night.

Despite what Sheryl had said, Mia didn't consider this a

date at all. It wasn't even two friends meeting up for coffee, because Mia wouldn't go as far as to suddenly define her relationship with Lou as friendship.

"Hey." Lou gave Mia a limp-wristed wave.

"Sit down and let me get you a coffee," Mia said.

"Thanks."

Mia headed to the counter and glanced at Lou while the coffee was being prepared. The way she sat there slumped over was in total contrast with how Lou usually carried herself. It struck Mia and made her consider how luminous Lou looked every other day of the week.

"Here you go." Mia put the coffee in front of Lou. "Nothing like a cup of Pink Bean coffee to perk you up."

Lou cradled the mug in her hands. "I feel like I said some impertinent things last night."

"You did nothing of the kind," Mia was quick to reply.

"I asked you out." Lou gave an incredulous chuckle.

"After you told me how *objectively pretty* I was, so there's nothing wrong with that. You eased into it." Mia wasn't sure Lou was up for a joke, but she didn't exactly know how to handle this situation, so she went for it anyway.

"Oh Christ. Don't remind me." Lou examined the contents of her cup of coffee.

"Good to know you've changed your mind about how I look then. That'll teach me to be so smug about myself all night." She had a big smile at the ready for if Lou dared to look up.

"I don't mean it like that, Mia." Lou glanced away from her coffee cup. "Surely you know why we can't go out."

"You're the one who asked." The coffee didn't seem to be perking up Lou at all.

"And you're the one who said to ask you again when I was sober," Lou replied snippily.

Was this about Mia not saying yes immediately? Not jumping at the chance to barge through the door to forgiveness Lou was leaving wide open? "Yes, and here we are. Both of us stone cold sober."

Mia could tell Lou was warring with something in her head. She could guess pretty easily what that would be. She tried her warmest, most symmetric smile. Just to see if it would unsettle Lou more. To test a theory.

"I enjoyed talking to you last night. I really did. And maybe we can be friends. I don't know. We can hang out, I guess. But I can't go out with you," Lou said.

"Would it really be such a hardship to share a meal with me?" It wasn't so much the sting of rejection that got Mia's hackles up, but that she was starting to get sick of being cast in the role of villain. If anything, she'd believed last night would have at least coaxed Lou's thoughts about her in a different direction.

"No, I mean, we can have dinner. But as friends. I wouldn't want you to think I was interested in anything more than that."

"There really isn't much chance of me doing so, Lou. Trust me, you're making that very clear." Mia leaned over the table, making Lou lean back. "But for the record, if you'd asked me again today, I would have said yes. And to take matters even further, I think we would have fun on our date. Because I get the distinct impression that, in spite of yourself, you actually quite like me. And that's the real problem here."

"So what if I like you? Sure, you're attractive. Any fool can see that. And you're nice to me. *Now*."

"Fine." Mia pushed her chair back. She didn't feel like this right now. This was ten steps back in whatever it was they were to each other now. "As long as that's the only way you can see me, then there is nothing between us. No date and no friendship either."

"Please." Lou's voice shook. "Don't go." She dragged her own chair closer to the table, as if to give the good example. "I overreacted. I'm prone to doing that sometimes."

Mia pulled her chair closer again. It was too hard to walk away from Lou in the state she was in right now. It would have made her feel like a coward.

"Why don't we hang out today? I could do with a greasy breakfast." Lou straightened her back for the first time since she'd arrived in the Pink Bean.

Was this Lou asking her when she was sober? And did it count when she was clearly so hungover?

"If you don't have plans, of course," Lou added.

"I go by Annie's Bookshop every Sunday. She always has a new recommendation ready for me."

"What are you reading now?" Lou glanced at the Jane Quinn book Mia had cast aside when she had arrived. "Is that one of Jane's?"

"It's research now, I guess. If I'm going to be working with them… I can hardly sell coffee in their shop without having read one of her books." Mia leaned over the table. "Jane has quite the loyal following. I honestly had no idea. There's so much we could do with that in the shop."

Lou shook her head. "You might have to up your powers of persuasion. Jane isn't too fond of the public eye. And that's putting it mildly."

"How would you put it non-mildly?" Mia was intrigued.

"She doesn't like people very much."

Mia chuckled. "I truly couldn't tell when I met her, but now that you mention it, I've been going to that shop for years and I've hardly ever seen her."

"So it wasn't a coincidence that I ran into you there on my way to my, er, hot date?" Lou flashed a smile at Mia.

Mia shook her head. "You did make Annie question me, though. The way you were skulking near the entrance until I left. She asked if we'd had a one-night stand gone bad."

It was Lou's turn to shake her head.

Mia searched for a sign of something on Lou's face. She obviously disapproved of what Annie had implied. "Does this mean you're suggesting we spend the rest of the day in Newtown?"

"If you like." Mia huddled over the table. "We could catch a movie this afternoon, if it won't be too traumatic for you to return to that particular cinema."

"Meredith was the one hung up on me, remember?" Lou leaned over the table as well and their faces were as close together as they'd ever been. "As long as you promise me you won't be called away for a work thing."

"I just had breakfast with my bosses. They said something about dinner at Kristin's parents. I don't think they'll need me for that."

"Speaking of dinner, I need to be back in Darlinghurst by seven for dinner at Phil and Jared's tonight."

"Ah, the two gays who were always so friendly and then mysteriously turned on me."

"I'll let them know you're actually not too bad."

"Just in case you're measuring their friendship by where they get their coffee after you told them about me, they still come here." Mia ventured a smile. Could they crack a joke about this already? Perhaps it was the only way past the thing that stood between them.

"It's okay. I gave them permission." Lou had a sly grin on her face. "And just so we're clear. This is not a date."

"Just hanging out," Mia confirmed. "Are there any rules I should abide by? I wouldn't want our hanging out to inadvertently turn into a date just because I cracked a smile at the right—or wrong—time."

"Just keep the flirting to a minimum," Lou said. "Shall we go? I'm starving."

## Chapter Twenty-One

Lou hopped off the bus after Mia. If she'd been alone, she would have gotten an Uber, but Mia insisted on taking the bus because she was showing Lou around her neighborhood and bringing her into her life and that couldn't be an authentic experience if they didn't take at least one bus.

They walked from the bus stop to The Larder, next to the cinema where she'd spotted Mia a few weeks ago, when she had still been so full of rage.

Mia ordered a salad but Lou needed fatty foods and the feeling of something really solid in her stomach after last night's excesses. She devoured her eggs benedict with avocado, while Mia scoured the newspaper she'd bought for the best movie they could watch together afterward.

"Don't tell me you're a blockbuster girl," Mia said, looking up from her newspaper. When she glanced at Lou like that, with that grin on her face, her eyes so clear and kind, Lou forgot she was actually Mia Miller. She was the woman she had drunkenly asked out the night before. God, the wave of anguish—followed by one of nausea—that had washed over her when she woke up, head banging, and realized she had.

"If I have to see one more superhero movie in my lifetime, it will be one too many." Lou put down her fork and considered whether to share this information with Mia. Why the hell not? "My ex was a comic book nerd and she dragged me along to every Marvel and DC movie that has come out in the past years. There have been many, and I hated almost all of them. Give me a French film with Isabelle Huppert any day of the week instead."

"Do I detect a touch of snobbery?" Mia put the paper down.

"It's not snobbery. Seeing a great movie is one of the biggest pleasures in life, but they don't seem to make many good ones anymore these days. Especially in America. It all seems so aimed at the lowest common denominator. Is it snobbish to want more than that for my entertainment?" Lou had given Meredith a similar rant during their date, which Meredith had gone along with. It was kind of a test to see if some of their preferences—and ultimately their personalities—would match.

"God no. I fully agree with you. And I'll raise you one. I once went on a quest to find the last ten movies Isabelle Huppert starred in, then watched them all in one week. With subtitles, of course."

"I'm impressed." Lou grinned. "And a little surprised."

"Why surprised?" Mia grinned right back at her.

"People who look so *objectively pleasing* as you do usually like the more commercial films." Was she flirting again? No wonder Mia had been blowing hot and cold at the Pink Bean earlier. Lou would too if she kept getting mixed messages like this.

"There we go with the objectivity again," Mia said. "I'm not that interested in anyone's objective opinion on how I look. I would like to know what you personally and totally subjectively think about how I look." Mia fluttered her eyelashes and cocked her head.

Lou felt a flush rise from her neck to her cheeks. "I think you know."

Mia sunk her teeth into her bottom lip and shook her head. "I don't."

"I asked you out, Mia. Under the influence, when my inhibitions were totally lowered and I allowed my instinct to take the reins." She pursed her lips, as though saying it was hard, while it was actually pretty easy, especially when she was staring at Mia's pretty face. "I think we both know I find you attractive."

"You're not so bad yourself." Mia held up her hands. "But I do think we've just entered the realm of very conscious flirting. I won't try to cast blame on who started it, but I think we should retreat. We are just hanging out, remember?" Mia followed up with the widest smile she could muster.

"Just find us a snobbish movie to watch already." Lou detected a tingle in the pit of her stomach.

Mia pored over her newspaper again. Lou watched her and just the simple act of gazing at Mia as she read filled her with an inexplicable, perhaps even obscene given their past, amount of joy.

———

"Charming, but hardly a masterpiece," Lou said when they exited the cinema.

"Give me your extended review later, we have to hurry." Mia touched her shoulder and guided them through the small throng of people in front of them. "Annie's will close soon and I haven't stopped by yet. She'll worry about me.

And what message would it send if I didn't go in and buy a book the Sunday before we're about to go into business together?"

"I'll forgive you the work talk," Lou said.

"My work is so mixed up with my pleasure. We wouldn't be able to talk about anything if I weren't allowed to bring it up."

Annie's was just a few minutes' walk away. Then Lou's phone started ringing. She delved it out of her purse and examined the screen. "Oh, great."

"What's wrong?"

Lou showed Mia the phone screen while she let it ring, as if Mia should know what a phone call from Angie did to her, how much it irked her.

"Let me guess, your ex?" Mia asked.

Mercifully, Angie hung up and the phone stopped ringing. Only to start blaring again a few seconds later.

"Do you want me to pick up?" Mia asked.

"What?" Lou held the phone to her chest.

"I won't be untoward, I promise." She arched up her eyebrows. "Come on. That kind of insistence needs to be dealt with. Otherwise she'll never leave you alone."

Reluctantly, Lou handed Mia her phone.

"Lou's phone. Mia speaking. How can I help you?" Mia said.

A brief silence.

"No, Lou's in the shower right now. Should she call you back?"

Lou shook her head. Angie's incessant calls had been irritating her, mostly because Lou didn't have anything left to say to her, but this was perhaps a bit too much. Angie was not the kind of person, especially not in the state she was in now, to take a phone call like this in jest. Lou would probably pay for this later.

"Okay. I'll let her know you called. Have a lovely Sunday." Mia hung up and handed the phone back to Lou.

"She said she'll call back herself. No need for me to give you a message."

"Oh Christ. I can just imagine her right now, fuming, steam coming from her ears."

"What's her deal? Didn't you break up months ago?" Mia asked while they started walking again.

"She keeps calling me. She even calls my mother. I tell her to stop. She does for a while. Then she has a bad weekend, one during which she misses me and sees the error of her ways, and starts calling again. As if a phone call is what it takes to get me back." Lou shook her head.

"So it's really over between you?"

"It couldn't possibly be more over and done with. I gave Angie so many chances and, one by one, she screwed them all up." Lou glanced at Mia from the corner of her eye. "I think I'll just remain single like you for the foreseeable future." They arrived at the bookshop and Lou regretted being there already, because it would halt their conversation and she suddenly found she had a lot of things to talk about with Mia.

"Mia and Lou." There was a strange note in Annie's voice. She emerged from behind the counter and kissed them both on the cheeks. "My saviors."

"Does that mean I no longer have to pay for my books?" Mia asked.

"If I don't have to pay for the five lattes you will serve me every day," Annie retorted. She seemed more alive to Lou than when she'd last seen her. Like she'd found the spring in her step again. She turned to Lou. "Can you imagine Mia and me in this shop together? I have an inkling half of the Newtown lesbians will take up reading print books again just to impress the cute barista."

Was that a pang of jealousy Lou detected coursing through her? It wouldn't surprise her if Mia was the resident heartbreaker of Newtown. She knew very well a lot of lesbians hung out here, and she wasn't liking the mental image of Mia being hit on by a slew of them.

"Please, Annie. I hope you're not about to make this deal so you can parade me around for my looks. I can guarantee you're setting yourself up for major disappointment," Mia said.

Annie gave Lou a look that Lou deciphered as wanting to say: *Can you believe that girl?*

"What have you got for me today, Annie?" Mia asked, changing the subject. "Actually, I'll take one of these as well." She glanced around the shop. "Ah, there they are." Mia walked to a shelf in the furthest corner of the shop that had a sticker on it with *Lesbian Romance*. "Oh yes, the sequel to the one Sheryl lent me." She turned to Annie. "Now that I've started on Jane's books, I'm not stopping until I've gone through them all."

She brought the book she had picked to the counter. "You really shouldn't hide those in the corner. You should make a big display of them."

"You try telling Jane that," Annie said.

"Maybe I will," Mia replied.

"Sparks will fly in my old shop. I look forward to it already," Annie said.

"I would very much like a front row seat when that conversation takes place," Lou said.

They chatted with Annie a little longer until another customer came in—heading straight for the Lesbian Romance shelf, making all three of them follow the woman with their eyes until it became uncomfortable. They paid for their purchases and Mia and Lou stood on the sidewalk again.

Lou glanced at her watch.

"You have to go?"

"I have time for one drink, then I'll Uber back to Darlinghurst. Traffic should be okay on a Sunday evening."

"How about a glass of top notch vino at my place?" Mia asked.

"Not sure about the wine, but I would love to see your place."

"Come along then." Mia held out her arm in a way that suggested Lou hook hers through it. She did and she felt a distinct frisson of excitement as she walked the street like that on the way to Mia's.

———

One wall of Mia's small flat was covered in books, which prompted Lou to say, "Only last night you claimed you couldn't read Jane's books. Today you bought another."

"It's research now. For work." Mia stood next to her fridge. "How about some organic lemonade?"

Lou nodded. "But you're enjoying the one you're reading?"

"I am. There's something so escapist about it. I'm there with these characters falling in love. As you might have sussed, I'm usually too snobbish to read romance, but I'll happily admit I'm enjoying Jane's book greatly. Even the naughty bits. It only took a small amount of effort to actually get over myself, and think about the characters that she created, and who now also live in my head, as actual fictional characters. It's not that hard when they're about twenty years younger than Jane and Annie. It's fiction." She screwed the lids off two bottles of lemonade and brought them over to what was supposed to be the lounge area, but was really only a small two-seat couch, a tiny coffee table and a television.

"My mother has a few of them. I don't know if she's actually read them," Lou said. "I'm sure I can find a few at home. I'll need to give them another chance."

"Sometimes we all judge too quickly and too harshly." Mia sat down next to Lou. "Anyway, welcome to my humble abode."

"It's so small." Perhaps it wasn't polite to say, but it was all Lou could think when she glanced around.

"I know, but only this week there was another article in the newspaper about how Sydney real estate prices are still rising this year. This is the best it's going to get for me until they go down again."

"Maybe if you make a huge success of the Newtown Pink Bean, you'll get a raise."

"I've only just finished my trial period," Mia said.

During the brief silence that fell, Lou's phone started ringing again. "You've got to be kidding me." She fished the phone out of her pocket. "It's her again," she said on a sigh.

"She did say she would call back." Mia held out her hand. "Do you want me to have another go?"

"No. I'll just turn it off." Lou pressed the off button hard, as if the pressure she applied could be felt by Angie in Brisbane. "I don't want to think about Angie for the rest of the day. It's been such a nice one." She smiled at Mia. "What was your last relationship like?"

Mia huffed out a chuckle. "Brief."

"That's not very descriptive."

"Yet it says all there is to say about it." Mia leaned back and brought the bottle of lemonade to her mouth. She even looked sexy when she drank. Lou wondered if the effects of a vicious hangover included increasing sexual thoughts about the woman she had drunkenly asked out the night before.

"I don't mean to be coy." Mia said after she finished swallowing. "I'm just not much of a relationship person. I've tried, but, I don't know. I think I'm just not really made for them. I'm happy on my own. When I meet someone I like, I tend to ask them out. We have a good time for a while. Then it organically comes to a halt. That seems to be the pattern."

"And you've never asked yourself why?" Lou sat up. She didn't want to miss a breath of Mia's answer.

"I have, but I stopped doing that after the umpteenth time things ground to a halt. I'm thirty-three. I figure this is how I am, how I'm wired."

"But what happens? Do you lose interest?"

Mia filled her cheeks with air and shook her head as she slowly let the air puff out. "No, I think it's safe to say it's usually the other party who loses interest in me."

"Somehow, I find that hard to believe."

Mia just shrugged.

"I'm not going to push you, but I just want it noted that I'm absolutely convinced you're not telling me something. You're holding something back."

Mia slanted her head. "Maybe that's the whole problem." She gave an unconvincing smile. "It's not the first time I've heard someone say that to me. If you hold back long enough, people will eventually lose interest."

Lou was glad this wasn't a date. That they were just *hanging out* and getting to know each other better. When Lou went on a date, she looked for signs of the other woman being a suitable mother. Even though she knew she was getting way ahead of herself when she did, that was one of her criteria. If this had been an actual date with Mia, she would seriously need to consider the possibility of not going on a second one because of what Mia had just said. She was clearly afraid to commit, and therefore didn't stand a chance against Lou's scrutiny.

"Why do you hold back?" Lou had to ask.

"I may appear all confident and rid of my past and all of

that, but that is exactly because I never disclose certain parts of me. You'd be surprised to find out how many women take it as a personal affront when you refuse to bare your entire soul to them. Complete honesty is a big thing in a relationship, or so it would appear."

It looked as though Mia was deflating right in front of Lou's eyes. "Are you referring to the bullying? To your father?"

"Bingo." Mia's voice was but a whisper.

"You've never told anyone?" Lou's eyes grew wide.

"It's not exactly a good sales pitch when you're trying to seduce someone."

"No, of course not, but afterward, when a relationship deepens, there's time to disclose the more unsavory parts of the past. We all have them. None of us are perfect and we all need forgiveness for something. If not from someone else, then at least from ourselves." The fact that Mia had never addressed her past with anyone made Lou believe she hadn't forgiven herself at all, despite sometimes hinting at it—and appearing very together about it all most of the time.

"It's how things are," Mia said, then fell silent for a few seconds.

Lou kept quiet in order to let Mia gather her thoughts and perhaps talk about what she had never talked about with any of her exes.

"Micky is the only person I talked to about it in all these years, and that's only because of you." Mia's voice broke. "I would never have confided in her if you hadn't told me who you were."

It was sounding as if Mia had needed Lou to turn up in her life. Even though Lou was convinced that, in the comparison of their suffering, she was and would always be the clear winner. The victim. The damaged party. The wronged one.

But now, she sat next to Mia in her tiny flat, and another

layer of Mia's bravado was stripped away. Mia had essentially told Lou how lonely she was—how lonely she made herself—and Lou wasn't so sure about her superior level of suffering anymore.

"You're the one who got the job at the Pink Bean. I was just going about my everyday business, teaching yoga, and spending too much of my hard-earned cash on coffee I could make myself." The air was getting so dense in this flat, Lou needed to lighten up the atmosphere a little.

"Maybe it was an act of fate that brought us back into each other's lives." Mia mumbled. "The universe knew we had unfinished business. You left Brisbane. I started hunting for a new job after I got sick of working for *the man*. And boom, here we are. Talking about the very thing that has marked us both so much."

"Do you believe in fate?" Lou couldn't keep her eye on Mia's face all the time, but she did notice that, after that short moment of extreme vulnerability, she was starting to put herself back together again.

Mia shrugged. "Not until now." She followed up with a smile. "Don't you have to go?" She pointed at the clock on the opposite wall.

"Oh, shoot. I'm going to be late." Lou put down the bottle of lemonade that had been empty for a while but which she had been toying with. "Let me see how long it'll take before I can get an Uber." This meant having to switch her phone back on. Before she did, she glanced at Mia. "I really wish I could stay."

"I'm sure I'll see you around." Mia rubbed her palms over her jeans. "Might even run into you tomorrow."

"Will you come to my 6 p.m. class?"

"I might."

Mia's non-committal tone drove Lou slightly crazy. Perhaps she had to take the initiative here. No, she knew she did. They'd spent a lovely, rather intense afternoon together. Lou had seen yet another side of Mia Miller. If she knew anything at all, she knew she wanted more.

"Would you still say yes if I asked you out now?" She wasn't entirely sure it was a good idea, but Lou had learned to follow her gut, and she knew that if she didn't ask, she would be kicking herself all the way back to Darlinghurst for not having the nerve.

"Try me." Mia leaned back on her elbows. The hem of her t-shirt rose and a sliver of skin was exposed.

"Mia Miller, would you like to have dinner with me?"

"I would." Mia's voice was forceful now.

"Good. My house. Wednesday evening?"

"Whoa… I'm not sure I'm ready to meet your parents just yet."

"They're on holiday. I have the place to myself."

"I'll be there with bells on then." Mia rose, while Lou switched her phone back on. A slew of messages came in alerting her to the missed calls from Angie. She could get an Uber in five minutes.

Lou stood awkwardly by the door, unsure of how to say goodbye, not only to Mia, but to the unexpected afternoon they had spent together.

"See you soon." Mia took a step in her direction, put her hands on Lou's shoulders, and kissed her on the cheek.

―――

"You asked her out?" Phil said. "Twice?"

"It's been an eventful weekend," Lou said. She was glad she had this evening with her friends to gain some perspective on her date with Mia.

"I did not see that coming," Jared said.

"To be perfectly honest," Lou said, "neither did I."

The twins were staying at their grandparents' tonight, so Lou couldn't count on them to distract the conversation. It was just her, her two friends, and all the questions they would surely have.

"Does that mean we can be nice to her again?" Jared asked. "It's been a bit awkward going to the Pink Bean."

"Oh, stop it, Jared," Phil said, while stirring something in a saucepan. "How did this come about?" They were all huddled around the kitchen island together, where Lou had sat many times since coming back from Brisbane. First to lament the breakdown of her relationship, then to vent over the return of Mia Miller in her surroundings, and now to tell them she had asked Mia out.

Lou could be completely honest with these two. Perhaps even more honest than she was with herself. "We had a pretty grueling chat during which she told me her side of the whole bullying story, but that's not even really the point, although I'm glad I know about it. It's just that, ever since then, since she sat in my living room and told me these things, I haven't been able to stop thinking about her. I didn't want to admit it to myself. Of course, I didn't. But I'm attracted to her. And not just because she has the looks, which, let's be honest, she does. But because she dared to look me in the eye, no matter how hard it was, and I saw that she was someone totally different to the bully I knew. And then we got chatting at a party and we hit it off and I was drunk and now I'm sitting here, after a wonderful afternoon in her company. So I asked her out. Again."

"So this will be a real date, with all the intentions of any old regular date behind it." Jared waggled his eyebrows.

"I'm not sure I know what you mean." Lou smiled at her friend. Of course, she knew, but if he was giving her a hard time, she was surely allowed to give him one back.

"You're not exactly a serial dater, Lou. And you just had

a less-than-good experience with that Meredith. And, well…" Phil stopped stirring in his saucepan for a second. "You're looking for, er, more."

"I think you might be getting ahead of yourself a bit there," Lou said, even though the same thought had crossed her mind. She couldn't help it. "Yes, it's a date, but at the same time it's *just* a date. What about you guys' first date? Surely you didn't turn up with the intention of having Yasmine and Toby one day."

"That was a long time ago," Phil said.

"Yes, we were still young and beautiful then," Jared said. "These days we have our lesbian friend over for dinner and we have to live vicariously through your thrilling adventures in love."

"Don't be so dramatic, babe. There's a time for everything in life. This is our time to be parents. I wouldn't want to go back to being twenty-five and single. This," he held up the spoon, "is so much better. By the way, dinner is ready."

They sat to eat and, aside from a few stories of what the twins had been up to, and the unwittingly funny things they'd said since Lou had last seen Phil and Jared, the conversation kept gravitating back to Mia, and Lou's upcoming date with her former nemesis.

"The hot ones are usually the ones with the most difficult character," Jared said, "that's why I had to settle for Phil." He blew his husband a kiss.

"And I for you, my dear."

"But maybe it's different for women. I mean, you're pretty hot, Lou, and you're the kindest, sweetest person I know. Maybe women *can* have it all."

"Come off it. Looks don't have that much to do with it in the end. Yes, I think Mia is hot. But that didn't mean a thing to me when I first saw her."

"You come off it," Jared said. "Looks do matter."

"Well, yes, but not as much as you would think. Plus, it's not because I find Mia good-looking that anyone else would."

"We both think she's very pretty," Phil said.

"Okay, fine, she's pretty. All I was trying to say is that I've seen beyond her pretty face now, and that's what matters to me. I would never have been attracted to her if I hadn't."

"She's a totally different type than Angie, though," Jared said.

"That's exactly my point," Lou said. "I don't believe much in types and instant attraction and all of that, and I wouldn't want you to think that I've decided to go on a date with Mia just because she's my type or because I find her physically attractive. I asked her out because, despite our past, I really like her. She moves something in me. And I need to find out what it is."

"Dear Lou, I would never suspect you of such shallowness," Phil said. "And you'd better have room for dessert."

## Chapter Twenty-Two

"What's with the smirk?" Jo asked her when Mia arrived at the Pink Bean on Monday morning, a full ten minutes before their shift started.

"What smirk?" Mia tried to paint as innocent a look on her face as she could muster.

"The insufferable one plastered across your face," Jo said.

"Josephine, I have no idea what you're talking about. I'm just happy to be spending the morning with you, my fellow barista and dear friend. That's all there is to it."

"You can say what you want, but you haven't fooled me for one second. I might not have been able to make it to Robin's birthday party but Caitlin told me all about how you and Lou have suddenly become inseparable."

Mia turned her grin into a triumphant smirk. She didn't even know where she got the energy to wind Jo up like this. She'd been up half the night, trying to divine more meaning behind Lou asking her out than there perhaps was. She'd also been reading the two Jane Quinn books. She didn't have any trouble shoving Jane and Annie from her mind during the juicy parts, but easily replaced the two romantic leads with her and Lou in the story line.

"Okay, I'll tell you, but don't go telling anyone else, okay?"

"Not even Caitlin?"

"I just don't want everyone around here talking about it and giving us funny looks."

"And by us you mean you and Lou?"

"We're going on a date. She's invited me to her house for dinner. Nothing has happened. It's just a date."

"Oh, I'm sure it is just a date." Jo stopped what she was doing for a second. "So you managed to set aside your differences from the past?"

*Good question*, she thought. Had they? Could they ever? All she knew was that she had allowed Lou to stare straight into her soul for a brief minute the previous afternoon. A peek into her inner world that she hadn't afforded anyone else ever before. And then Lou had asked her out. "We're trying to," she said and headed for the door to turn over the Open/Closed sign. "Time to open up shop. Are you ready for the grumpy Monday morning crowd?"

———

For the first time since she'd started working in the Pink Bean, Mia was truly looking forward to Lou coming in for her daily dose of caffeine. She was curious about how Lou would act—and perhaps a bit scared that she might have come to her senses and would revoke the invitation to dinner.

When she and Amber walked in the door, Josephine said, "Go on, take five. Have a chat with your upcoming date."

Mia shot her a *shut-up* look, even though she was happy for Jo's generosity.

"Do you have a minute?" Mia asked Lou after she'd

ordered. She felt suddenly much shyer, an altogether different emotion from the ones she'd felt every previous time Lou had walked in. She was feeling insecure as well. Perhaps even questioning of Lou's motives, now that an actual date had been set.

"Morning," Lou said, and the smile she gave Mia was so wide and sunny and doubt-erasing, that Mia felt compelled to do what she'd done the night before when Lou was about to leave. She put her hands gently on her shoulders and kissed her on the cheek, not caring or even wondering whether that was appropriate. Besides, from what Sheryl had told her about the Pink Bean, many romances had sprouted here, so Mia figured a chaste kiss on the cheek might even be encouraged.

Lou took a step back and regarded her funnily, her eyes slightly narrowed. Perhaps the cheek kiss had surprised her.

"Do come to yoga tonight," she said. "Even though I'm not supposed to focus more on one student, I'll pay special attention to your posture."

Mia had brought her workout gear, but now she was definitely going. Still, she had to ask. "Are we still on for Wednesday?"

"Of course. I'm looking forward to it, although I may have slightly overestimated my cooking skills."

"Take out is fine with me," Mia said.

"No, take out won't do." Lou stepped closer again. "Is there anything you don't eat?"

Mia shook her head, sank her teeth into her bottom lip, and just looked at Lou. It was liberating to do so, to feel this chemistry crackle in the air between them, to be aware of the promise of what could be—a sentiment she had become a bit jaded about the last few years. Because she always knew it would be gone soon.

"Bring a bottle of wine of your choosing then."

"Psst," Jo whispered from the counter. "Here's your coffee, Lou."

"I'd best get back to work," Mia said. "See you soon." As she made her way back behind the counter, she made a mental note to ask if she could stay over at Kristin and Sheryl's on Wednesday night.

"I can keep a secret, Mia," Jo said. "But sparks were flying all over the place, so you're lucky it was just Amber and me in here and not Micky with her big mouth otherwise the entire population of Darlinghurst would know about your date within the next twenty-four hours."

———

Mia ran a hand through her hair, then rang the bell. It was odd that she'd actually been to Lou's house before.

The door flew open, then there she stood. Her hair was loose and even though it was no longer out of the ordinary to see Lou out of her yoga gear, Mia still did a double take, because Lou was wearing the sort of dressy tank top that was designed for one purpose only: seduction.

They kissed on the cheeks, but Mia couldn't resist keeping her hands on Lou's bare shoulders for a fraction of a second longer than necessary.

"Smells nice in here," Mia said when Lou escorted her into the kitchen. She remembered how her stomach had growled that day she had come here with Lou, and how Lou had offered to make her a sandwich. She'd never thought she'd come here for an actual dinner—just the two of them —one day.

"It's only pasta," Lou said. "Tell you the truth, I haven't done a lot of cooking since I moved back home. Both my mother and father love to cook, and they also very much love to feed me. This is one of my dad's recipes. Very easy to make and, hopefully, equally yummy when made by his daughter." Lou sounded as though she was blabbering a bit.

"I look forward to it." Mia's nerves were making themselves known in her stomach, so she wasn't very hungry. She handed Lou the bottle of Pinot Gris she had brought. "I hope this goes with your dish."

"Perfect, and cold as well. The glasses are in that cupboard over there."

Lou had set two places at the dining table and they sat with their glasses of wine.

"I don't know about you," Lou said, "but I'm feeling a little awkward. How shall we get past this initial awkwardness then?" She held up her glass. "Do you think this will do the trick?"

"It might be a little awkward, but it doesn't mean we can't enjoy it. I'd like to guess that the reason why it's a little unnatural is because we both very much want to be here." She held up her glass as well. "I hope you haven't had second thoughts."

Lou shook her head and clinked her glass against Mia's.

"Good, because you were the one who started flirting with me on Sunday afternoon, despite first telling me not to flirt with you."

Lou just gave a small smile. "I'm truly sorry I had to rush off like that. Especially because of the nature of our conversation. I've thought about it a lot since then."

"You mean my inability to keep women?" Mia smiled. "It was very strange to be asked on a date after admitting to that. As if you were trying to prove a point."

"Is that what you think?" Lou shook her head. "I didn't ask you out to prove a point, Mia. I swear to you. I asked you out because we had such a good time and…"

"Yes?"

"I don't quite know how to put it into words," Lou said.

"I just knew I wanted to spend more time with you. Because of how I feel when I'm with you now that the dread has gone and the shock of seeing you again has worn off." Lou cocked her head. "Is that enough of a reason?"

"What was I thinking asking for a reason in the first place?" Mia hoped the smile she gave Lou was convincing enough. Because she wanted to be here, despite her insecurities, and all the events that had led them to sitting opposite each other at this table. The air between them was rich with something intangible but exciting already. And Mia wondered if it would be there as well if they hadn't known each other as teenagers.

"Any news on Annie's?" Lou asked, changing the subject expertly.

They talked about the Pink Bean and bookshop merger for a while, how they were ironing out the kinks in their agreement and trying to come to terms that every party could be happy with, even though compromises would have to be made on both sides. It was a safe topic, but also the very thing that had instigated their increasing closeness.

After they finished their first glass of wine, Lou served dinner, which smelled and looked great. In spite of the wine, nerves were still getting the better of Mia's stomach. Why did dates have to include eating anyway? Was it to closely scrutinize a potential love interest's table manners and base future decisions on them? It seemed ridiculous to Mia as Lou set a plate of food in front of her.

"Linguini marinara," Lou said. "Enjoy."

"It's really good," Mia said after swallowing a bite. "You should cook more often."

"Next time it'll be your turn, obviously." Lou grinned at her.

"Next time, huh? Aren't you getting a little ahead of yourself?"

Lou shrugged. "Story of my life, really. In my mind, I'm always a couple of steps ahead. It's how I'm wired. How I survive in this world."

"That sounded a bit grim toward the end." Mia loaded her fork but didn't put it in her mouth. She regarded Lou instead. She could come out with the weirdest phrases at times, which was fascinating as well as puzzling.

"Well, for example, I can't put all the blame of my failed relationship onto my ex."

"Any more phone calls, by the way?" Mia asked.

Lou shook her head. "In the end, I as good as thought our relationship to death, if that makes any sense. As soon as Angie started deviating from the plans I had for our future, the clouds of doom started gathering above our relationship. Clouds only I could see and had to make her aware of. Even though it goes against everything I've been taught as a yoga teacher. You know, live in the moment and all that."

Mia tried to follow Lou's train of thought, but couldn't. "I'm not sure I fully understand."

"You may notice I sometimes have a really hard time translating what I think and feel into words. Especially when I'm nervous." She grabbed her glass of wine. "This helps."

"It's okay. You don't have to explain."

"I want to. Let me try again." Lou took a deep breath, put her glass down, and said, "Let me give you another example. From the very beginning of our relationship, which started when we were both still quite young, Angie and I decided we wanted to have children. We talked about it a lot. I even started seriously researching it, right around the time we started to grow apart. Because I thought that if I took some resolute steps in the direction of our future, she would follow suit, but it had the opposite effect. She only started working more. I started pushing more. She pushed back. In the end, you can't tell a grown-up what to do. And I wasn't being very subtle about it, either. She kept saying we had time, that women have their children much later these days, and that it would be better to wait until we were more financially stable and so on. Until I woke up one day and realized we didn't share the same dream anymore. I guess that was the hardest part."

Mia wasn't quite sure what to say to that, or how the conversation had suddenly drifted toward Lou's failures and dreams. Was she meant to share hers? Would it make her come across as shallow if she didn't have any tales like this to tell—because she didn't. "Not that I'm the expert, but relationships fail for so many reasons and they're often much more complex than we can see at first sight."

"She was good to me. Angie, was." Lou refilled their glasses. "She got me, you know? Not a lot of people do. We were good together for a long time. Until we weren't, I guess. But I should really stop going on about myself, can I ask you a question?"

"Isn't that what tonight is all about?" Mia threw in a crooked smile.

"How do you recover from relationship after relationship ending? And often not on your terms? What does it do to your self-esteem?"

Mia drank to take some time to think. Lou had stopped eating, so she left her fork untouched as well. "First of all, I learned not to let my self-esteem depend on my relationships. Second, I haven't had that many affairs that deserve the term relationship. And when those relationships ended, it was often more a relief than it was painful for me."

"Because you felt more comfortable hiding?"

Mia shook her head. "I don't know. But I'm hardly the exception. I know a lot of people my age who are single and happy, who have short-lived affairs, casual sexual encounters, who live a more unattached life. This is not the fifties anymore."

"And thank goodness for that." Lou narrowed her eyes. "I have so many questions for you, Mia. I'm beginning to think our talks might be somehow therapeutic for me, or at least cathartic."

"Shoot." Maybe that was what they were to each other more than anything else; a means to put the past behind them once and for all.

"Does your father know, er, you're a lesbian? From what you told me, he didn't do very well with anything that didn't fit the norm."

"God no. My mother left him when I was nineteen, during my first year at uni. I hadn't come out yet. I was still dating boys. I saw him a few times after they divorced, but I felt increasingly uncomfortable around him, so I stopped seeing him. I was an adult. I never told him, so as far as I know, he doesn't know. Or maybe he does. Maybe he found out somehow, and that has contributed to his decision to never seek me out. Since I broke contact, he has never been in touch, has never tried to fix our broken ties."

"Personally, I can't imagine life without either of my parents," Lou said.

"So I see. You live with them."

"I know." Lou scoffed. "Exactly how pathetic does that make me look?"

"It just makes you look like someone who gets on really well with her parents. It only has positive connotations in my mind."

"I don't do very well on my own," Lou said in a musing tone. "The thought of coming home to an empty house every night fills me with dread."

"It's not too bad. And I speak from experience."

"Have you ever lived with anyone?" Lou asked.

"When I was at university, but I've lived on my own for the past ten years."

Lou glanced at her but didn't say anything. From the way she furrowed her brow, Mia could tell there was something on her mind.

"You can ask me anything, Lou," she said, and meant it, because she had given away much more of herself to Lou already than she had to anyone else. She could give more. Lou had that effect on her now.

"I do have another question, but it's one of those questions that can really kill the mood on a first date, because it's not really a first-date question at all. And I'm really not looking for a wrong or right answer. I'm just curious. Perhaps too much so."

"I will reply as truthfully as I can." Mia shuffled around in her seat. Lou really was trying to psychoanalyze her tonight, it seemed.

"Do you want children?" She didn't flinch when she asked it, and it seemed to Mia there was very much a right or wrong answer—especially because of what Lou had said earlier about why she and Angie had split.

"That's a big one."

"I know. I kind of feel sorry for asking it already."

"Because you're afraid of what I'm going to say? That it won't be what you'll want to hear?"

"Because I'm thinking about a million steps ahead of what I should be thinking right now."

"And you don't want to waste your precious time on someone who doesn't want to have children with you."

"Which is ridiculously presumptuous on a first date." Lou held up her hands. "I withdraw the question. Can I do that?"

Mia chuckled. "You can. But that way you won't get to hear my answer."

"I don't want to hear your answer, Mia. It doesn't matter

right now. We're having a lovely evening. I was out of line. It's none of my business what you want to do with your life."

"Maybe I'll tell you on our second date, then."

"If you want to go on one after all this." Lou hid her face behind her hands.

"Well, you've already instructed me to cook you dinner, so I guess it's going to happen either way." Mia got a lot of glee out of winding Lou up.

Lou shook her head. "I really exasperate myself sometimes, what with this knack I have for saying the wrong thing at the most inopportune moment."

"This wouldn't be a very successful first date without any mishaps. Besides, your question really wasn't that bad. It just shows me some of your personality and leaves me with absolutely no doubts about what you want in life." She smiled softly. "And let's just say I might very well want some of the exact same things."

"So I didn't scare you away?" Lou asked, peeking through her fingers.

"No, just as I didn't scare you away when I told you about my lack of commitment in relationships last Sunday."

"If you put it like that, it's a miracle we're sitting here at all."

"I won't argue with that."

"I'm having a really good time, though, despite you having barely touched my food."

"I was just following your example." Mia peered at her still half full plate.

"Clearly, I'm too nervous to eat much."

"Same here."

"And there's something else." Lou's voice grew a little sultrier.

"What's that?" Mia tilted her head.

"I've wanted to kiss you ever since I let you in the door."

## Chapter Twenty-Three

*Did she really just say that?* Lou glanced at the bottle of wine and it wasn't even empty yet. She hadn't had that much to drink. She must really want to kiss Mia then, if her desire sat so readily on the tip of her tongue. She glanced at Mia, examining her reaction after she'd spoken the words and Mia's face could not reveal anything but the truth about how she really felt about Lou's statement.

Mia smiled. Not her usual easy smile, but a less brazen, more subtle one. She didn't say anything, just pushed her chair back, got up, and stood next to Lou, holding out her hand. Lou rose.

Mia brushed Lou's hair away from her ear with her hand, and whispered, "The thought had crossed my mind as well."

Their date had moved to the next level. And despite that dream Lou had had, and the hours she'd spent analyzing it, and the one or two times she had intentionally brought Mia into her sensual fantasies, Lou had not dared to dream that their very first date would go in this direction. She hadn't deemed it possible. Not with their history. She had believed they would talk and talk, and then talk some more. But now it appeared that all the things that needed to be said for them to reach this stage had already been said. Lou knew enough. She'd known as soon as Mia had kissed her on the cheek when she arrived. That thing between them that was becoming less of a mystery every minute they spent together. Lou knew it was because of who they once were to each other that they stood in this position here tonight. Getting ready for their first kiss. It wasn't fate or destiny or coincidence. It was redemption. For both.

Just because of that, it was implied that Lou had to instigate, that she had to be the one to open the door to what was to follow. And she wanted so much more. *She* had asked Mia out. Mia had come to *her* house. Now it was up to her to kiss Mia. And to set in motion whatever would happen next. It had to be her, even though Lou didn't much feel like being pushed into that role just because of their past, and she instinctively knew Mia was much better at that sort of thing than she was.

Yet, Lou led the charge. She brought her hands to Mia's pale neck, and savored the moment her skin made contact with Mia's, relished the tiny shock running up her spine, the shiver rippling from her fingers to her sex. She slanted her head, eyes wide open, and pressed her lips to Mia's. The sky didn't come falling down, nor were their pasts erased because of the magic of their lip-lock, but it felt so damn good to kiss Mia, that Lou pulled her near, opened her lips to Mia, and let her in as much as she could.

Mia had her hands in Lou's hair and they both pushed themselves closer toward each other, even though their lips had reached the pinnacle of closeness already. Mia moaned into Lou's mouth, indicating that she wanted more too. That this kiss meant the same to her. That she needed it as much as Lou did.

Was Lou really going to take Mia Miller up to her room? She had changed the decor, but it was the same room she had slept in as a teenager, the very same room she had cried bitter tears in because of the woman she was kissing now. The thought didn't stop her. On the contrary.

"Let's go upstairs," she said.

Mia didn't say anything, just gave Lou a prolonged stare, as if to ask, *are you sure?* But of course Lou was sure. Even though she had no idea where this would end, what it would do to her, or if it would survive one night together at all, she knew without a shadow of a doubt that she wanted to take Mia to bed.

She tugged at Mia's hand and guided her up the stairs, down the landing, to her bedroom, where a bunch of unopened boxes still remained stacked in the corner, because she hadn't had the nerve to fully face up to the failure that leaving Brisbane represented. But Brisbane or Angie or any of those words that had rolled out of her mouth during dinner were no longer of importance. When it mattered, Lou *could* be completely in the moment. She could pay no attention to the past and stop thinking a dozen steps ahead, and just be in the here and now. And that here and now was Mia Miller in her arms in her room.

Mia didn't glance around; she only had eyes for Lou. Eyes that seemed to devour Lou, as if she'd already taken off her clothes. The top Lou had worn to impress because it accentuated her shoulders. Her jeans that clung hotly to her thighs.

They stepped closer again and fell into another passionate lip-lock, even more probing and daring than the one downstairs, if such a thing was even possible, and then Lou's hands found a way underneath Mia's shirt, and she touched, she believed, the exact patch of skin she had seen exposed last Sunday when Mia had leaned back on the couch. And even if it wasn't, in her head it was, and it was perfect. This moment was perfect, because they had only kissed and the excitement of the pleasure to come was running deep within her flesh, until the intensity of their kiss dropped and Lou remembered her responsibility.

This was her house, her room. Mia was her guest, but also her former tormentor. She had to give permission at every turn. Or did she? What would happen if she just let go? If she let things take their natural course, because between two people, there was always a natural order of things, and with Mia, Lou felt that to lead would go against her nature.

"Please," she whispered. "Take charge." She looked Mia in the eye, those dark wells of mystery and unexpected kindness and, tonight, anticipation.

Mia gave the tiniest of smiles followed by an almost imperceptible nod. She stepped closer so there was not a millimeter of space left between their bodies, forcing Lou's hands to land on the small of her back. She brushed Lou's hair away from her neck again and kissed her above the collarbone before making her way up to her lips again. Lou leaned her head back. This was touching of a totally different order than what she and Angie had engaged in at the end of their relationship. It was electric and maddening and of the kind of depth Lou didn't think possible two people could reach on a first date.

But there she stood, trembling under Mia's touch, wanting nothing more than her clothes to be torn off her. Her skin to be covered by Mia's. Mia's hands all over her. Because this was all about Mia. Even if her first date with Meredith hadn't gone awry, Lou would never have gone this far with anyone else after a first shared meal together. This was only possible with Mia. As though the demons of her past could only truly be expelled this way and their memory was, at the same time, necessary to propel her into Mia's arms.

When they broke from their kiss, Mia tugged at Lou's bottom lip with her teeth, then smiled wickedly as she let go. Something had changed in her glance. Perhaps because of the permission Lou had granted her by bringing her up here and asking her to take charge.

Mia cocked her head and regarded Lou for a moment. What was she thinking? Lou wanted to know every tiny thought running through her head. The first time with someone was all about guessing—and second guessing—and exploring and trying this and that. She was glad she had put Mia in charge. From what she'd told her, Mia must have had many more first times with other women than Lou had. She was doubly glad she'd had the nerve to whisper those words to Mia because there was something about her that telegraphed her desire to do so, but that in this particular situation, deliberate permission had to be given. The words had to be said. Of course, it could also very well be that Lou was imagining all of this, that her mind was racing because her body was about to go into overdrive—and the body always follows the mind and vice versa.

Mia brought her hand to Lou's neck and stroked the hollow of it with her thumb, then ran it over her collarbone.

"These shoulders," Mia half-mumbled.

Lou barely understood her, but it seemed Mia hadn't spoken those words with the intention to be understood. They were words meant to express desire and to bridge the gap of their current position to the next, which Lou was hoping fervently would be on her back on the bed.

Mia leaned in to kiss her again and Lou, with her hands still on Mia's back, pulled her closer, making her intentions known again. Their breasts met with too much fabric in between them and Lou thrust a knee between Mia's legs as a new swell of desire rose through her.

She had to draw back. Had to stop herself from flinging herself onto the bed, dragging Mia with her, pulling her on top, somehow tearing their clothes off in the process and getting to the next stage. Because she had dreamed of seeing Mia naked. Hesitantly at first, not fully allowing herself to give in to the image that was forming in her mind's eye. But what good was imagining anyone naked? What purpose did it serve except indulging in a quick whim after dark? The difference between the idea of someone naked and that person standing next to you, skin and soul bared, was night and day. And Lou wanted it all. She had her hands on Mia's skin. She no longer had to use her feeble powers of imagination.

She'd been so elated to find Mia in her yoga class last Monday, and she had done as promised and paid special attention to Mia's posture, especially when she bent forward in downward-facing dog, and Lou had cast many a glance at her shapely ass. She let her hands wander down to said ass now, cupped it in her hands. Something she'd definitely wanted to do a few times during yoga, but that had, of course, been impossible.

While Mia's fingers dragged excruciatingly slowly over Lou's neck and shoulders, Lou got a good feel of Mia's behind. But, again, there was too much fabric in the way. Why had she allowed Mia to take charge again? Sod it, her hands were going in. If all Mia was going to do in the next few minutes was drive her crazy, slowly but surely, until she was putty in her hands, Lou would have to show some initiative. She slipped her fingers beneath the waistband of Mia's jeans and met more fabric.

Mia's thumb crept up Lou's jawline, coming to rest on

her lips, pushing Lou's bottom lip down. Lou looked her in the eye and saw only desire. Desire, and anticipation, as though Mia was preparing for something. Revving herself up. As though the outcome of this night was wholly unexpected to her and her mind was racing to catch up with what her body was already doing. The opposite of Lou. She was the very opposite of Lou in so many ways, and all the more enticing for it.

Was she thinking about all the ways she could drive Lou crazy before she stripped her naked? Or was she simply bewildered by the situation she found herself in ? It was impossible to tell, and there were too many possibilities running through Lou's head for her to fully enjoy this moment. She took a deep breath and kissed Mia while her fingers slid underneath her undies.

Mia's breath hitched and her hands dropped down to Lou's jeans, flipping open the button. Mia's hand delved in freely, and her fingers stroked Lou over her already drenched underwear. It was a light caress that didn't last nearly long enough, only gave Lou a taste of what was to come—and gave her a good idea of what kind of person Mia was when you handed her the reins. She was going to pay for it with mounting desire. There would be no quick tearing off of clothes and tumbling onto the bed naked. Perhaps Mia felt she had something to prove and this was how she chose to do it, although Lou suspected this was just how she was. And Lou could lament it all she wanted, but deep down, she loved it. She loved every exquisite second that Mia made her wait for anything.

Mia now trailed a fingertip over Lou's belly, just above the line of her panties, up to her belly-button, then down again. Lou's skin was on fire where Mia touched her, but her mind was still racing. Because she hadn't been able to explain this to herself yet. The very fact that Mia Miller was standing in her room, driving her crazy.

Mia bent her knees and pulled Lou's pants down in one go. Lou stepped out of them in as composed a manner as she could, but the sudden gesture had tripled the pace of her heartbeat.

With surprising agility, Mia pushed herself back up and stood face-to-face with Lou. "Sit on the edge of the bed," she said in a tone that Lou wouldn't dream of contesting—not that she wanted to.

She was still wearing her panties, but she would gladly spread her legs for Mia. If that was what she wanted. Lou sat down, knees held close together. She glanced up at Mia who had started to unbutton her shirt. With a casual flick of the shoulder, she sent it to the floor and stood in front of Lou in her jeans and bra.

The sight made Lou's throat constrict with desire, made her clit almost burst with lust. What was it about Mia that turned her on so much? She shook the thought off. The time for analyzing had passed. Mia curled her hands behind her back, as though she was about to unhook her bra. She kept her hands there and stared at Lou with a small smile playing on her lips. Then her hands returned, as if she'd had second thoughts—even though Lou was convinced it had been Mia's intention all along—while her bra remained in place on her body.

Mia took a step closer and simply put both her hands on Lou's knees. It was all Lou needed as a command to spread her legs.

Lou's panties were so wet that the fabric clung to her sex, as though caressing her where Mia didn't want to—yet. She leaned back on her arms and glanced at Mia from under her lashes. Even though she could never have imagined any of this, it still felt as if all of it was meant to be. As if the minute-by-minute play that was happening in her bedroom tonight had been written in the stars for them, by them. Every last thing of it, the tiniest emotion it stirred in her, felt right.

Mia sank, kneeling in between Lou's legs, as though about to worship at an altar. Just her presence there was enough to ratchet up Lou's desire by a few levels. While part of her longed to lie on the bed with Mia, naked, stroking each other's soft warm skin, discovering each other in a more conventional way for a first time, the truest part of her preferred this. The rest would follow later. As far as stating intentions went, Mia kneeling in between her legs was far superior to gently tugging off each other's clothes and exploring what lay beneath.

Mia ran a finger along Lou's inner thigh. Up and down, then it moved to the other, trailing circles and complicated figures on her skin, making every last hair on Lou's body stand on end with anticipation. At last, Mia's finger stroked along her panties again, but still too far away from where Lou really wanted it. Not for long though. It skated down, avoiding her clit, to run along her throbbing lips. Lou couldn't see between her legs because Mia's dark hair obstructed her view. She couldn't stop herself from bringing one hand to Mia's head and running it through her hair. Lou hoped it would spur her on to rip Lou's panties off her, so she could bare her most intimate self to Mia, and get the growing arousal humming in her blood taken care of. This was beginning to feel more like torture than foreplay. But Lou was only getting what she had asked for.

Mia's finger lightly circled her clit—still over her panties. Oh yes, definitely torture.

Lou strangled a moan in her throat. She might have asked for this but she wasn't going to beg for more. She trusted Mia to take her where she needed to go, to follow a pace that was bearable, to bring Lou to the cliffside of desire and then catch her on the other side.

If Mia kept circling like that, Lou's arousal threatened to catch up with her, spill over the edges she was skirting now, and tip her over prematurely. But Mia was smarter than that. Her finger retreated, then hooked itself underneath the hem and pulled away the wet panel of her panties.

Oh Christ. Too much air down there, not enough in her lungs. And the thought of Mia's stare. Was she just looking? Yes. Nothing stirred in the room, there was no sound other than the ferocious beating of Lou's heart in her ears, that mad drumbeat pumping more blood to her swollen clit. Seconds passed. Minutes. Lou didn't know. Her brain had become incapable of measuring units of time. Everything blurred together. The first time she had seen Mia again in the Pink Bean and how it had felt like a punch in the gut—a punch Mia had never meted out. Mia Miller had never touched her, had only ever hurt her with words—words spoken by a tortured teenager. Words that hurt them both equally. The first time she was able to see Mia as the person she was now. The soft touch of Mia's lips on her cheek when she'd kissed her goodbye last Sunday. And now this. The upcoming soft touch of Mia's lips elsewhere. It was the beginning of something. Lou had no way of knowing what exactly, except that it would include much needed healing for both of them.

Then Mia's mouth pressed against Lou's naked lips, against her throbbing clit. It was just a kiss, light and gentle, yet it was so much more. It held in its touch both forgiveness and new beginnings. In its intention, both the expulsion of demons and the will to drive Lou crazy. The last bit was working really well. So well that Lou let a moan escape from her throat. It burst out of her, the way the tears had done when she was a teenager, unstoppable and giving voice to something unspeakable.

Once Mia put her tongue into play, Lou was lost. It was all too much. Her hand slipped from Mia's hair and she leaned back on both her elbows, throwing her head back, enjoying Mia's touch, her now insistent tongue on her clit, running along her lips, dipping inside, driving her mad. Because that was what Mia had done from the very beginning, long before Lou had even had the smallest inkling of it.

Mia's hand pressed against Lou's thigh where she held Lou's panties at bay. It was an exquisite sensation, almost equal to the touch of her tongue on her pussy, because of the action it implied. Because of how that hand had been responsible for setting Lou free, for showing all she had and she was to Mia, for allowing her into that most intimate of spaces between her legs, to do to Lou as she saw fit. And it was the surrender most of all that got to Lou as she thundered toward climax. Until Mia stopped. Insufferable stillness in the air for a split second. And then, the touch of a finger against the rim of her pussy. It didn't linger, but pushed inside, high and deep. Another moan escaped from Lou's throat. Mia was taking all she had, and giving the utmost pleasure in return. Mia started licking her clit again while she pushed her finger high inside Lou. All the dots connected. Even Lou's own groans and moans spurred her on, put her right back on that road to orgasm, made her muscles tremble and her blood sing. Then she was coming. She was coming at Mia's hands and tongue. It was the end of one road and the beginning of another. It was a moment of extreme joy that could never be taken from her or erased from her memory. It was something she'd needed since that moment in Mia's flat, when Mia had opened up to her without Lou even trying very hard.

Then Lou uttered two words she never thought she

would. "Oh, Mia." She crashed through her arms and let the back of her head fall onto the mattress. She brought her own hand to where Mia's thumb had stroked earlier in the hollow of her neck, as though she could feel her there, as though that was where it had all begun.

## Chapter Twenty-Four

Perplexed, Mia sat between Lou's legs. Had this really just happened? Had her life taken another crazy turn yet again, and was Louise Hamilton the source of it again? She pushed herself up from between Lou's legs and took in how she lay spent on the bed. She was so beautiful she almost looked like a vision to Mia, like someone unreal descended from the heights of heaven or, perhaps, brought up from the very depths of hell to play a trick on her.

Mia rushed to Lou's side, wanting to touch her, not only because of the pull between them, the electricity crackling in the air when their skin touched, but also because she wanted to verify whether Lou was real. To confirm that the woman from whose body she had just demanded orgasm, and who had gladly accepted Mia's tongue and fingers, was an actual person—was, in fact, Louise Hamilton.

"Are you all right?" Mia asked as soon as she came face-to-face with Lou again. She brushed the back of her hand over Lou's cheek and felt the flush that burned on her skin. That skin of which she could never really describe the color, except perhaps now, with the rosy red of her blush mixed in.

It looked like liquid honey, like gold set on fire, like an expanse of silken softness Mia wanted nothing more than to disappear in again and again.

"You're still wearing your top," Mia said, as she dragged it upward and ran a finger over Lou's belly.

Lou turned on her side, pressing her hot belly against Mia's. "Because you made me."

Mia wondered if Lou's words held any deeper meaning or if she could take anything she said at mere face value. Or was it what lay beneath it all that made this so thrilling?

"I'll make you take it off now." She shot Lou her warmest smile.

"You'll have to help. I seem to have lost all muscle power in my arms."

"All that yoga and so easily wiped out." Mia pressed a kiss on Lou's cheek and with a very inelegant, clumsy movement, maneuvered the top over her head.

"My top for your bra," Lou said. She ran a finger over the cup of Mia's bra. "You're such a tease, by the way."

"But you loved every second of it." Mia brought her hands behind her back and let her bra drop down. The air on her skin and Lou's gaze on her breasts intensified the throb between her legs. A pulse that had been building since Lou had told her she'd been thinking about kissing her earlier downstairs. Mia had come here for dinner, perhaps more of a kiss goodnight than an exchange of pecks on the cheek, but she'd never imagined this. Not only because she didn't dare, or because it would surely lead to disappointment, but because she had no right. She had absolutely no right to find herself in Lou's bed tonight. Yet here she lay. Her lips smelling of Lou's most secret perfume, her ears still ringing from Lou's orgasmic cries.

"I can't tease you the way you teased me," Lou said. "It's not in my nature."

"The need for teasing has long passed." Mia kissed Lou on the lips. "Let me know when you've regained your strength. I'm going to need some of that muscle power."

"Taking off your jeans would surely help." Lou's eyes seemed glued to Mia's chest. Entranced, she ran a wide circle around Mia's nipple.

"I'll see what I can do." Mia tried not to tear herself away from Lou's caress while she slipped out of her jeans, but her skin lost contact with Lou's fingertip for a brief moment, a moment during which all the cells in her body screamed for her to reestablish a connection immediately. As though Lou touching her was the new norm. As though her body could no longer live without Lou's touch.

Mia had taken off her underwear in the process, and she lay on her side facing Lou, who was still wearing her bra and soaked panties. But Mia relished the thought that she hadn't seen Lou completely naked yet, that there would still be something to discover later.

"Yes, this has done wonders for my strength." Lou became bolder, zeroing in on Mia's nipple, her finger hovering, then touching down lightly, leaving it hard and wanting.

"I can tell." Mia was about to run out of words, or perhaps the strength to speak. She needed wordlessness now, a silence that could consume her and speak for her at the same time. She scooted closer to Lou, wanting to feel much more than that fingertip that already stirred so much in her. Even though Lou had asked her to take charge, Mia had no desire to steer this moment. This was Lou's moment to express herself, to show to Mia, but most of all to herself, what desire looked like when it took hold of her. Was her desire for Mia as great as Mia's was for her? Mia didn't think it possible. But perhaps that was because Lou's finger was beginning to drive her crazy, push her past a point of no return, a point where no other thoughts were possible.

Mia examined Lou's face. She was biting her bottom lip as if she was concentrating really hard, or contemplating her next move, or perhaps even doubting it. And this was the beauty of moments like this, when you didn't know someone else very well yet, but there was promise between you, and the thoughts in the other woman's mind were still made up of possibilities instead of disappointments. Mia hadn't made it past many moments like this, and the times that she had, she'd felt herself retreat as soon as she'd crossed that invisible line. What if she was still ugly on the inside? What if she had somehow found a way to rid herself of any outward signs of the juvenile monster that she had been, but what if remnants of it still loomed deep inside, waiting for the right moment to pounce?

As she lay with Lou, Mia couldn't believe that about herself. Because Lou was not the sort of person who would look into Mia's eyes, drag a finger over her skin the way she was doing now, and forgive her, if she still had the tiniest smidgen of that past evil inside of her. It was the one thing that Mia believed with all her heart and that she hadn't been able to believe with anyone else before—because they didn't matter the way Lou did.

Lou's finger dived deeper, traced a circle around her belly button, then plunged straight between her legs. Did she know that Mia was more than ready for her? That a few strokes of those delicious fingers would most likely be all it took. Because Lou was gorgeous and it had aroused Mia greatly to feast on her earlier, but that was not what this was about. It wasn't even about quenching the desire that was so visible in Lou's eyes. It was all about saying yes without words that could fail or hold different meanings and could be misinterpreted. Their bodies were saying what their lips couldn't. There was so much truth in one body acquiescing to another, no other statement, no other way of granting forgiveness, could ever speak with more clarity.

Mia kept her gaze on Lou's face and she saw a small smile appear as Lou encountered the wetness between Mia's legs. Mia spread her legs, lifted one knee up so Lou's hand had full access. There would be time to experience the pleasure of seeing Lou disappear between her legs, her face leaving Mia's field of vision as it approached Mia the way Lou's hands were approaching her now, all candor and lust and the willingness to please. But that was for later, because right now Mia had a more immediate pleasure on her mind.

Lou drew the same kind of circles she had drawn around Mia's nipple earlier. Wide at first but quickly zoning in, quickly leaving Mia breathless.

Lou's lips had parted in concentration or perhaps sheer delight and Mia thought it a great privilege that she was allowed to read Lou's reactions off her face like that, that she was granted access to this part of her as well. By the time they went to sleep, she'd have seen it all. Lou would have given her everything. But before that, Mia had to give back. Because Lou was looking at her face, having diverted her gaze from her chest. She was staring into Mia's eyes as if she was looking for that one last ounce of truth she may need.

The circling motion of Lou's finger became more insistent and Mia had trouble keeping her eyes from screwing shut because the intensity was too much to bear open-eyed. Was this it then? She asked herself in those moments when all went dark before her eyes, before it all blazed into an expanse of white as another jolt of about-to-be-met lust shot through her. Was this the beginning of love? Was she falling in love with the most unlikely person? Was she showing herself a way she had never followed before? Thoughts like these spurred her on to keep her eyes open and to meet Lou's gaze as her climax approached, searching for the answers in the expressions of Lou's face.

But then Lou's finger abruptly stopped circling and slipped inside Mia, making her cry out in a heartfelt moan.

Lou's smile widened and it was the kind of smile that connected with every fiber in Mia's body, that ignited a fire in her every cell. To see Lou smile like that. To be the source of it.

Lou fucked her slowly, staying away from her clit, but it didn't matter, because Mia was already well on her way to orgasm. She'd been waiting and the points of her body that were now graced by Lou's touch reacted much more excessively, because they marked the spot where Mia's physical pleasure was originating. They could have been any spot that Lou touched inside her, they might just as well have been Mia's lips as they drew into a smile, or her knee that stood up straight, or her hair that kept falling into her eyes. None of it mattered, because Lou's finger was doing exactly what it had entered Mia for. It was delivering her from any last thought, any last belief that the old Mia might still exist. Because the Mia with Lou's finger inside of her, and with Lou's intentions connected to hers through that very finger, could only be the person she already knew she had become. The person she had always been.

Mia bucked her hips to meet the last of Lou's strokes as the fire inside her swelled. Mia cried out again and Lou took it down a notch. But Mia kept bucking, wanting to feel Lou's finger inside of her, wanting to ride out this climax and prolong the meaning it imprinted on her brain.

When she finally allowed Lou to withdraw her finger, tears streamed down Mia's cheeks and, as she let her legs fall shut, she buried her face in Lou's long hair.

Lou threw an arm around her and held her close. She didn't say anything. Didn't ask if Mia was all right. They were still in the space of wordless atonement, of their bodies speaking the ultimate truth. Mia knew her tears said more than her words ever could.

———

"Don't you have to get up?" A voice whispered in Mia's ear. "I think you forgot to set your alarm."

"What?" Mia opened her eyes and looked into Lou's face. She burst into a smile immediately.

"The Pink Bean will open soon. Don't you have to be there?" Lou smiled back. Her hair was all over the place, half of it covering her face, some of it tickling Mia's shoulder.

"What time is it?" A slight panic took hold of Mia, but not enough to deter her from the utter beauty of this moment, of waking up next to Lou—even though it was a bit of a rude awakening.

"Six fifteen." Lou quirked up her eyebrows as she said it.

"Looks like I'm going to be late." She couldn't stop staring at Lou.

"That's your reaction? What if I see it as my duty to inform Kristin about the laxness of her employee's time-keeping?"

"Then I would have to change your mind. Give you a really compelling reason not to." Mia threw her arms around Lou's neck and pulled her close. "And I have no time to waste." She sank her teeth lightly into the flesh between Lou's neck and shoulder and as a shudder of morning lust ran up her spine, she caught a glimpse of all the times she would pull Lou close like this, all the mornings they would wake up next to each other, all the times they would share a joke between them and distance themselves more from who they used to be.

"Not compelling enough," Lou said into her shoulder. "Not nearly."

Mia pushed Lou onto her back and straddled her, touching down with her pussy lips on Lou's warm belly. "If you keep this up, you'll be the reason I'm late and you'll have no claims to make about my loyalty to my boss." Mia bent down and kissed Lou on the nose. "Besides, both Jo and Kristin know about our date. They're probably already blaming it on you. And rightly so." Mia kissed Lou on the lips.

"They all know?" Lou asked as soon as they broke from their kiss.

"Jo read it off my face and Kristin is too smart not to know."

"There are no secrets in the Pink Bean." Lou smiled up at her. "I kind of knew that all along."

"I'll try to do a better job in the Newtown branch. We'll have a strict non-gossip policy."

"You can try, but don't forget I have a direct line to any antics you might be up to. Just one phone call to Annie is all it will take." Lou narrowed her eyes. "I think I might ask her to keep tabs on all the hot lesbians who come in for coffee when you're there."

Mia chuckled until her eyes fell onto the alarm clock next to Lou's bed and it hit her what time it was. "I have to get a move on." In her haste, her foot got stuck in the sheet and she nearly tumbled to the ground, but Lou caught her and pulled her close by the arm.

"Last night was great," she said. "I want to do it again as soon as possible."

"Then I shall cook for you as instructed."

Lou shook her head. "No cooking will be required for what I have in mind."

"Well, well, well." Jo stood with her hands on her hips exactly the way Mia had predicted she would. "Look what the cat dragged in."

"I'm sorry." Mia painted the most innocent look on her face, though she felt far from innocent. "Is the boss around?"

"She went back upstairs after she came down to ask me if you'd turned up yet. Apparently, you didn't come home last night." Jo tilted her head and held up two fingers. "That's two strikes."

"Was Kristin pissed off about that?" Mia didn't realize she needed to have taken the time in between kissing Lou and being dragged upstairs to let Kristin know she wouldn't be staying at hers after all.

"If I were you, I'd prepare to get an earful later, my friend."

"You're pulling my leg. You are my evil barista twin. Kristin can be a bit uptight, but she wouldn't get upset about that."

Jo shrugged. "Only time will tell."

A few customers came in and they were busy for half an hour with no time to chat. Mia kept staring out of the window for any sign of Lou, who had promised to drop in before her first class of the day. Mia's heart skipped a beat when she saw Lou's familiar profile enter her field of vision, then make her way to the door, open it, and step into the Pink Bean.

"Good grief," Josephine said.

"What?" Mia glanced at Jo and noticed her shaking her head slowly.

"Must have been some date. You just looked as if Angelina Jolie herself just walked in that door."

"Someone much better than Angelina Jolie, wouldn't you

say?" Mia shot Jo a wink and the way she grinned back at her made it very clear to Mia that she'd been joking about Kristin's reaction earlier. This was the Pink Bean, after all. The Darlinghurst coffee shop where, according to Sheryl, many a lesbian had encountered true love.

"Hi Jo," Lou said, then gave Mia the most delicious stare.

"Christ, I think I need to go call Caitlin," Jo said. "Too much love in the air for me not to."

Mia flinched at Jo's mention of the word love. Lou hadn't moved a millimeter. She just stood there sporting a smile Mia still had to get used to having aimed at her.

## Epilogue

Lou couldn't keep her eyes off Mia, who was strutting around the shop as though she owned it, as though she had invented the concept of the bookshop and was the first person on the planet to ever extract coffee from a handful of beans.

This was Mia at her best, even though it was only one side of her, or one side where many of her good qualities converged into the display she put on today: warm, welcoming, confident. A smile so easy, so bordering on sultry it made Lou weak at the knees—because she knew what it looked like when it crossed over all the way to sultry. She had been on the receiving end of Mia's sultry smiles for three months now, and she didn't think she could ever do without them.

"I sure hope we did the right thing," Jane, who was standing next to her, said. "Not so much merging with a coffee shop and with people who clearly know what they're doing, but bringing such a young thing into our lives. Look at her, Lou. Your girlfriend is a live wire. And all that coffee won't help." Jane snickered. Lou had been standing next to her for a while and she'd made a game of keeping tabs on how many glasses of champagne Jane had consumed during that time. Jane didn't get out much, but when she did, and on special occasions like these, she went all out.

Then Lou lingered on the words *your girlfriend*. Mia was her girlfriend now. There really was no other way to describe her.

"I'm not sure I need that kind of excitement in my life," Jane continued. "I prefer a quiet life."

Lou smiled at her. "Don't worry, Jane. You don't have to come down to the shop if you don't want to."

"But what if I do want to, despite myself? What do you young people call it? FOMO?"

"Then come down and see what all the fuss is about, after which you can go back upstairs again and continue in your solitary ways."

Jane knocked back the last of her champagne. "This means so much to Annie. I think she feels she's got a second chance. She's reading even more than before. I think she really wants to have read every new book that comes in, in order to give the best possible recommendations. I told her it was impossible, but I have a sneaky suspicion it's her way of dealing with the change. Because it is a big change. She's so used to being in this shop on her own. Granted, she's much more sociable than I am, but she's quite solitary as well, in a way."

"Jane, come here." Sheryl ambled up to them, arms wide open. "Have I told you how honored I am to be in business with you?" She threw her arms around Jane and pulled her into a hug.

"About a dozen times already," Jane replied. "But you can keep saying it, if you like."

"I've even persuaded Lou and Mia to read your books. I think Mia has gone through most of them and Lou is quickly catching up."

"I shall be forever grateful," Jane said.

Lou recognized the tiny signs of retreat—the stiffening of the smile, the too-fast blink of the eye—in Jane. She was even more uneasy dealing with praise than she was dealing with people.

Lou left them to their conversation and found Amber and Martha chatting to Micky and Jo.

"All the things that have happened since I started work at the Pink Bean," Micky said. "No offense, Jo, but you worked there for two years before me and nothing spectacular happened. I show up, and boom!"

"Yes, Michaela." Jo gave her a round of fake applause. "You are the very reason for all the wonders of our world. I shall compose a song in your honor and sing it—"

Amber turned to Lou. "They're at it again. I think Micky misses Jo much more than she will ever admit. I've known Micky forever, but we don't have that kind of relationship."

"That's because you take everything so seriously, babe." Martha leaned into Amber. "Nothing is trivial in your world. I love that about you."

"Hello, friends." Mia slung an arm around Lou's neck. She held a bottle of champagne in her free hand. "Who wants a refill?"

Everyone held out their glass, except for Amber and Lou.

"We're both teaching tomorrow," Amber said. "Best keep it civilized."

Mia shook her head. "I was told those Sunday morning classes were meant to be taught alternately. This is young love you're standing in the way of, Amber." Mia kissed Lou on the cheek, then turned to Martha. "What do you say, Martha? Shall we start a petition against Sunday morning classes at Glow so we can keep our significant others in bed a little longer?"

Neither Amber nor Lou had expected the Sunday

morning classes to be such a success, but apparently quite a number of people like to begin their last day of the weekend with some yoga.

"Do you have any idea what time Amber wakes me up when she doesn't have a class to teach?" Martha shook her head. "I prefer it like this because she sneaks out silently and I can have a lie-in." She grinned at Amber.

"Don't worry, Mia. I promise you'll have at least one in two relaxing Sunday mornings with Lou soon. I'm very close to finding another suitable teacher."

"You've been saying that for weeks," Mia said. "I thought yoga teachers grew on trees these days."

"We're very particular at Glow." Lou came to Amber's rescue. "It needs to be a good fit."

"She's just looking for a second Lou," Martha said. "And that's proving hard to find."

Mia refilled Martha's glass, then said, "I can hardly argue with that, can I?"

Lou leaned into Mia a little closer, then let her gaze wander over the group she was standing in. She remembered going to Glow for the first time, being impressed with the teacher and the whole vibe of the brand new studio around the corner from her parents' house. So much had changed since then, not least of all the reintroduction of Mia Miller into her life.

"As if you won't be here bright and early tomorrow morning." Lou grabbed Mia's hand. Merging Annie's with the Newtown branch of the Pink Bean had been Mia's baby for the past couple of months. It would always be intertwined with Lou's memories of the beginnings of their relationship.

"Only because my bed will be empty, babe." She put down the bottle of champagne, turned fully to Lou, and curved her arms around her waist. "You will always come first." She flashed a smile that touched Lou deep in her core. A smile that said everything and that echoed all the ones that had helped erase the memories from Lou's mind about the other Mia she once knew, but who had long ceased to exist. So many new memories had been made since then and with every day that had passed, Lou had felt her own confidence grow.

Not only had she picked up the pieces of her life after her break-up with Angie, she had also faced herself, and the person she once was, the scared teenager who would always be a part of her, but who she could see as so much more than all the things she blamed herself for then. That girl had been her and she had grown out of her, but she had only fully become herself—the self she was now—once she had looked Mia in the eye and told her, in a clear and steady voice, that she had forgiven her.

"I know." Lou kissed Mia on the nose to loud howls and whistles from the others. Perhaps Jane had been right. She had no idea what she was letting herself and Annie in for by allowing this crowd into their shop and into their lives. For Lou, every single one of them had been a godsend.

## Acknowledgments

In these Pink Bean acknowledgments, I seem to have acquired the habit of taking stock or, at the very least, addressing the theme the book is about in relation to myself. But life has been so crazy these past few weeks (due to travel, deciding to move back to Belgium, and subsequent house hunting), I'm literally writing this thank-you note when this book should already be at the distributor.

Lack of time to ponder the book, of course, doesn't mean I'm not very grateful to everyone who has helped me with it.

First and foremost, I must thank my wife, who has had to deal with countless meltdowns of my overly dramatic self during the time it took to write *Water Under Bridges*, time which was mainly spent on the road and in countries very foreign to me. She deserves a million medals for that alone, but she also came up with the idea for this story. This once again proves that, in my world, no wife would equal no books.

Thank you to my editor and friend, Cheyenne Blue, who

does far more than edit my books (and has taught me that long-distance friendship is very much a thing.)

Thank you to my beta-reader, Carrie, whose advice on 'the scene' was greatly appreciated and convinced me to cut some long-winded sentences from a crucial moment in the book.

Thank you to all the valued members of my Launch Team, one of whom I met in person a few weeks ago. It turned into a wonderful afternoon and it made me want to meet every single one of you some day—if I should be so lucky.

Last but certainly not least, thank you, Dear Reader, for continuing to make all of this possible for me. Your messages, emails, and reviews cheer me up every single day—and get me through the ones when I don't feel very writerly inclined.

Thank you.

## About the Author

Harper Bliss is the author of the *Pink Bean* series, the *High Rise* series, the *French Kissing* serial and many other lesbian romance titles. She is the co-founder of Ladylit Publishing and My LesFic weekly newsletter. Harper is currently on a digital nomad adventure around the world with her wife Caroline.

Harper loves hearing from readers and you can get in touch with her here:

www.harperbliss.com
harperbliss@gmail.com